LEVIATHAN
AWAITS

LEVIATHAN AWAITS

Jamison Fussner

WESTBOW
PRESS
A DIVISION OF THOMAS NELSON

WestBow Press books may be ordered through booksellers or by contacting:

WestBow Press
A Division of Thomas Nelson
1663 Liberty Drive
Bloomington, IN 47403
www.westbowpress.com
1-(866) 928-1240

Designer- Samson Lucas Fussner
Artist- Joseph Garrett Fussner
Indexer- Soni Sully
Mary Mcmillan
Editor- Falinda Mcclung
Proof Reader- Angie Llewellyn
Author- Felic Jamison V. Fussner

ISBN: 978-1-4497-8673-1 (sc)
ISBN: 978-1-4497-8675-5 (hc)
ISBN: 978-1-4497-8674-8 (e)

Library of Congress Control Number: 2013903464

Printed in the United States of America

WestBow Press rev. date: 3/11/2013

CONTENTS

Chapter 1   Admiral Vladimir Voss's Story 1

Chapter 2   The Sitter & the Adventure 9

Chapter 3   The Briefing 14

Chapter 4   The Treasure & the Promotion 21

Chapter 5   Leviathan Arrives. 27

Chapter 6   Illustrations. 34

Chapter 7   Off to the Mission 42

Chapter 8   The Escape 50

Chapter 9   Leviathan Awaits 57

Chapter 10   The Vosses Ready for Russia 65

Chapter 11   Dragon. .68

Chapter 12   The Visit with the Russians. 86

Chapter 13   Leviathan Unites 92

Chapter 14   Anatoly calls for Queen Leviathan 99

Chapter 15   At Last 112

CHAPTER 1

Admiral Vladimir Voss's Story

I N THE SEA OF BARENTS, somewhere off the coasts of the Northern Islands, before the days of the great flood, where before the fountains of the deep were broken up which closed the accesses to the center of the Earth; the passageways were easily navigated by the largest of creatures, the Leviathan.

This behemoth traveler made his way through the chasm and caves even to the center of the Earth where the fires tempered their scales and flesh. They found their way through the flames to the other side of the Earth to a favorite city of refuge. This city was a place where the people worshiped them because of their size and ferocity. The fish in the lakes around the city were large and plenteous and being easily pushed into the traps the Leviathan herded them for the people to catch and even cooked them with a quick breath of their fiery nostrils. Although the people asked if they could cook their own fish because when the leviathan did it they were a little too well done for their liking. (But what would you expect from a creature that has sulfur for desert?)

In the days when the Leviathan were around there was a feast every night, slow cooking the fish on open spits seasoned with butterfat from the kine.

The ancient language of the Leviathan was still the language of this people, being untouched by the dividing and confounding of languages of the wicked nations of the Northern Hemisphere. But when the days of refreshing were over, back through the fires to the duties of the North they went. The ancient ones lived on the Earth for thousands of years before they came to this palace city under the seas: their foods were plenteous. They raised different kinds of foods in various places to accommodate their veracious appetites. North of the Barents Sea, the polar bears were raised in the great valleys of Magog, feasting on the seals coming through the ice, who were unsuspecting of the white bears looming over head. They plopped onto the ice to take a break from the icy waters. The bears would feast and fatten themselves on them for the feast of the Leviathan. Leviathan only took the larger older bears so the population of polar bears would thrive. A single Leviathan of behemoth proportions, from the great age they were, could eat as many as seven polar bears in one sitting. Herding them with his tail of a hundred yards long right up to his sharp terrible teeth, he plucked the larger ones out of the pack and with a single flaming breath cooked the large white bear right in and between his teeth. It was good that way; the long white hairs would be singed right off the hide. None escaped when the attention of the behemoth Leviathan was focused on his prey.

"Hey wait, wait a minute PaPa. How could an animal be as long as a foot ball field? What language is this you are speaking of? How do you know of the days before the flood? And and..."

"Anatoly!" PaPa Vladimir stated in a calming voice. "Anatoly, all of your questions will be answered in the rest of the story. Calm yourself and I will proceed and answer all of your questions."

"But PaPa you are leaving next week to go back to the Antarctic, and I won't see you again for who knows how long. Why did you not tell me of these things before? Does DaDa know of this? Why did he not..."

"Anatoly!" PaPa Vladimir stated a little more firmly. "Grandson, you are only two years of age."

"Two and one half year, PaPa".

"Yes, yes, now shush, your Father struggles with the autism you have, and doesn't see the brilliance yet. Your Father has not even listened to your outcries but responds to them instead. I will speak to him for you. As for my returning to work, this computer I bought is for our continued communication while I am working. I will email you every evening and speak to you by phone twice a week. Now Anatoly, how many languages do you know?"

"Well PaPa. I know German but don't speak it. Russian, of course. English only because that is all MaMa knows. Some Chinese, but don't practice writing it (Mandarin). Hebrew is very difficult and has similarities to Aramaic and..."

"Well!" PaPa Vladimir exclaimed. "You have been a busy boy. This new computer we are setting you up with will aid you with the other languages. I had all the latest language programs installed. And by the way, Anatoly, do not take this one apart. It is built the same as the others, and you cannot see the memory in this one either."

"Yes PaPa, I understand now." "As for this ancient language, Anatoly, my dream has been for you to rediscover this lost language that was confounded and made to be forbidden in many cultures. Just as Hebrew and other languages has been forbidden and forsaken through time. As for your other questions, I will be able to work out some details after dinner. I think I hear your Mother calling."

"But PaPa, now is better."

Vladimir stood and looked sternly into Anatoly's eyes, answering. "Yes, PaPa. I will be along directly."

As Vladimir walked through the doorway, Anatoly turned and saw his dinosaur collection on the shelf, after studying them for a short minute he grabbed a box from his closet shelf and with one scoop of his arm knocked them all into the box and put them on the closet floor, exclaiming, "These aren't all that big anymore." And he turned to go eat his chicken nuggets which is about all he would eat, that and apple sauce..

Dinner being finished, Anatoly got ready for bed. He could hardly wait for the story to resume. GrandFather knew where to pick up so as Anatoly would minimize his questions. Anatoly tucked himself in and pulled his blanket carefully over his mouth, so as to not waste another moment. Loosening the blanket he said, "Ready PaPa". Vladimir smiled, cleared his voice, and just began.

"The ancestors were behemoth because of their age. Some of the ancestors are still alive and since they never stop growing." Just then, Anatoly loosed his blanket a bit as if to ask a question, but Vladimir held up his finger knowing what the youngster was to ask....and said, "Yes, Anatoly, still alive." Anatoly knew the finger meant his questions would be answered and reminded himself he was not going to interrupt. As he listened intently, he sunk into the recesses of his mind and thought in full color pictures as to better remember every detail. Thinking sometimes in Russian and other languages racing through his mind simultaneously, the brilliance of his mind told him the story even before the words came out of PaPa Vladimir's mouth.

Vladimir continued: "Few Leviathans ever died or were ever killed nor could any harm them but one foe, the LORD himself. So the largest of the creatures were thousands of years old. They only had off spring every hundred years or so, and the babies were as big as men and as their scales were not yet tempered by fire. They did not get wings for nearly a thousand years or even legs and arms for nearly one hundred years. So the only time they were vulnerable at all to the wicked men of the North was when they were young. And the men of the North Country would seek them out diligently, because they greatly feared them and did not speak their language, or understand their intentions. The armies would go out with spears and habergeons of iron. But they were no match for a Leviathan of any size. They could not pierce their flesh with any weapons they could imagine, and if they got close enough, the great dragon's fiery breath would consume them. Even the armor they were wearing was not able to withstand the temperatures of the great Leviathan's flame. Their armor would be found in a heap of rubble.

The peoples of the North were ever pursuing, looking for the offspring, desiring to crush Leviathan from existence, not even knowing how many were left or when Leviathan was avoiding them. They were in the depths of the seas or passing through the heart of the Earth looking to go to the city of refuge. Nor did they understand as the Leviathan did, knowing and understanding the paths of the whole Earth and through the Earth, able to go to and fro in it or around it through the seas, the depths not an obstacle, plenteous food wherever they went understanding all creatures and knowing which were good to eat. Not fearing any, but the LORD himself. All would go to the city of refuge, but only after the harsh winters, for fear they would get trapped in the ice by the ever moving Earth and depths.

The beloved city might not be able to contain all Leviathan in existence through the long winters; some would have to stay in the caverns and passageways leading to the city, coming through the Earth. The young ones stayed behind in the North not able to withstand the fires of the journey and not being ready to temper their flesh. Even as a young Leviathan, they can breathe fire--not sustaining fire long enough for a lengthy battle, but able to defend long enough to escape. When the behemoth Leviathan returned to the North and discovered all their offspring slain, their wrath was (vastly fierce) in the city. Three great Leviathans made a plan of attack. All the inhabitants would have been destroyed with the city but a few used tunnels and escaped to the wilderness. The few survivors would have perished, but the few survivors called upon the name of the LORD. And the LORD answered and came and crushed the head of the Leviathan and fed them to the people of the wilderness. So the Leviathan went back to avoiding the people of North once again, and spending more years finding hiding places for their offspring where they would never be found again.

In the dark depths, where Leviathan frequently travel, they lit the way as they went, able to travel long distances under the sea, traveling to the bottom depths. Unable to harm them, high pressure atmospheres did not affect them. Traveling with great speed and agility, the greater their size, the faster they go, knowing the paths under the sea and across the lands even through the caves and chasms, sometimes traveling in lines as to pull along the smaller and the younger. They could travel to such depths, pulling them in their wake and waves that they made with their enormous bodies.

In their communication of complex yet simple language, they could plan, tell tales of days gone by, and talk of ancestors. They communicated as well underground, under water, above ground, and in the air. They understood as they talked of all the creatures and their habits. As to know their prey, they teamed together to herd any creatures they desired, of any size or speed. Man was never on their list of food, not fearful of man, but to avoid man. To hide and make men not to notice them. If they were cornered, they would defend themselves, by whatever means the situation dictated. Their defense was in their scales, so closely knit together air could not pass through. Nothing man could throw at them could harm or wound. Man would not understand the Leviathan wished to live in peace, as they did with the men of the South Country, the Antarctic region.

But the men of the North went their own way, not considering any creatures, only serving their own desires, their own flesh, and their own drunken feasts. Fighters gorged themselves with exotic foods. Wasting, ever wanting war. In the Northern region, the Leviathan never had rest from the wicked. To their own kind, the men of the North showed some respect. Not knowing any language but that which benefited themselves. They could have learned of the Leviathan, and their language, if one cared or even noticed. Instead, they went in the ways of their Fathers to destroy the Earth for their own desires, pursuing the largest of creatures for their own pride.

The Lord Visited Man And Gave Man Prophecies.

The Leviathan heard the prophecy that all mankind would be destroyed and the foundations of the deep would be broken up. They planned to escape, through the caverns and chasms. All must go. They separated into groups, to travel. They formed a plan to go to the land they loved. The pathways that were always so easily navigated might soon no longer be there. They would all head to the city, where the people worshiped them, through the center of the Earth. Only the ones large enough to travel through the fire would be able to go. Provisions were quickly made for the young to stay, planning to return to them, instructing the young to meet together in the depths of the great sea; not knowing if they would survive the cataclysmic event that was to happen on all the face of the Earth. They would be passing through the caverns coming out the other side, back to the city they loved, back to the people that understood them. As they planned, the Earth began to quake. The time came and was here.

Their plans were flawed; the time of the deep to be broken up came too soon, trapping some Leviathan in places without food, without resources of life. The ones in the lead pressed on, seeming as if not to care but sticking to the plan, they pressed on. Down to the depths, through the fires exploding, breaking up the great deep, some trailing behind, trying to catch up. Obstacles fell in their paths, all pressed on, unable to hear. Communication was difficult. Fires were loud. Almost as loud as the Earth's rumbling, the rocks fell: molten rock exploded. Folding their wings to their bodies and becoming projectiles, through the caverns they went, not able to rest, keeping their eyes on the Lead. The Lead was hoping many were following, making it through the old passageways, longing for that city that they loved.

They would make a new life there when things settled down. They would be able to travel to and fro again. It would be good to see the men that worshiped them; fish with them, feast with them. Leviathan know no pain and their hearts are like stone. The flakes of their flesh are joined together. They are firm in themselves they cannot be moved.

"His heart is firm as a stone as hard as a piece of the Nether. Sharp stones are under him; he spreadeth sharp pointed things upon the mire. He maketh the deep to boil like a pot ; like a pot of ointment. He maketh a path to shine after him. One would think the deep to be hoary. Upon Earth there is not his like, who is made without fear. He beholdeth all high things; he is a king over all the children of pride. In his neck remains strength and sorrow is turned into joy before him. His breath kindleth coals, and a flame goeth out of his mouth. None will make a covenant with you. None shall make him the servant. None shall find, none shall make a bank to pay these things."

And they chanted like sayings to themselves over and over as they passed through Sheol, through the quaking Earth they lifted themselves by changing their greatness over and over. The days passed over them, the ones behind, falling off. How many would remain? (The Lead thought.) You long for the city, aching change, taking no pain; their hearts are like stone, the flakes of his flesh are joined together. They are firm in themselves; they cannot be moved. His heart is as firm as stone as hard as a piece of the nether. Sharp stones are under him, his greatness. Who is made without fear, he is king over all the children of pride. Tirelessly they journeyed on 40 days and 40 nights that Earth did shake and Leviathan pressed on. He ever encouraged himself with bold talk of his kind."

By this time Anatoly's eyes were as wide as saucers, with his blankets tight on his mouth leaving a red mark below his nose. He saw PaPa was stopping for the night, and he threw the blankets off and screamed "Not here, not now! How many made it? Wait, did they make it? PaPa, please."

PaPa said, "Anatoly, tomorrow is another day. It is late. There is too much to tell. Good night Anatoly."

PaPa Vladimir firmly held the boy by the shoulders and laid him back down gently and tucked him in. Looking him square in the eyes, he quietly told him, "Close your eyes and practice your languages. Then maybe one day you can talk to Leviathan." Anatoly looked puzzled, and as if to be in a trance, closed his eyes, and relived everything he heard that evening in color.

CHAPTER 2

The Sitter & the Adventure

AFTER TWO HOURS OF SLEEP, Anatoly awoke, wide awake and got on the computer to learn more languages. He worked until the sun came up. There was a knock at the front door. "I know who that is," thought Anatoly. He raced for the front door. "I knew it was you." There standing in the doorway, blocking the morning light was Aryn Paige Davis, the sitter.

Though she liked to refer to herself as the nanny, Anatoly said she was too young to be a nanny, and he didn't need a sitter (in his mind). But he was always glad to see her. She thought of every day as an adventure.

She was a gangly looking girl but beautiful to the core, thin and wiry, and very athletic. Best of all, SHE HAD A CAR. They could go on great adventures, which kept Anatoly's mind active, as long as they were home before dark…that's when Anatoly's parents got home from work.

"Aryn, put your things down and come to my room," Anatoly stated excitedly. Aryn knew he had something big to tell her, because he was so excited. Anatoly began even before she got to his room. "I

must tell you of the secrets my PaPa Vladimir told me last evening."
With Anatoly's sharp keen mind, he almost repeated word for word
the events that unfolded the night before.

MaMa and DaDa Voss were awake, dressed for work, making
breakfast and coffee, when they heard a shriek come from Anatoly's
room. They ran to the room to find Aryn sitting on the edge of the
bed with her hand over her mouth. Anatoly was standing on the
chair over her waving his arms telling his story. Aryn looked up at
the adults springing into the room and exclaimed to them, "Oh! I
am sorry Mr. and Mrs. Voss. I got excited at Anny's story." Anatoly
looked back down at Aryn and pointing his finger at her face said, "I
told you, don't call me that, my name is Anatoly Vladimir Voss!"

Aryn looked back up at him and said "Sorry Anny," Instantly
Anatoly jumped on Aryn, rolling them back on the bed. Aryn
shrieked, fell back on the bed, and they both giggled. MaMa and
DaDa Voss smiled and turned toward the kitchen calling for Anatoly
to follow. "Come and eat your oatmeal. There is breakfast enough
for you too, Aryn." Softly MaMa said, "I am glad they are such good
friends."

Aryn cleaned for the Vosses on the days the maid was off. As she
was doing the dishes, Anatoly went to the front window to watch his
parents leave. As Anatoly climbed up on the bar stool, he exclaimed,
"They are gone now. We can go on an adventure, Aryn. I know
where Lafitte's gold was buried and we can retrieve it even today."

Aryn put the last dish in the dishwasher and putting her hands
on her hips, looking into Anatoly's eyes said, "You are not going to
get me into trouble again; we are not going anywhere. Besides, Mara
dropped me off, and I don't have the car today. Let's make better
plans this time so I know where we are going, and what you are
getting me into. Treasure, you say. Is this for real or are you using
symbolic reasoning to quantify your study of something? "

Anatoly took the dishtowel from her hand, neatly hung it on
the rod, and grabbing her fingers ,pulled her to his room. "Come
on, I will show you I am right. This is for real. I drew a map and
everything according to my calculations from Laffite's Journal!"

"Wait, wait," Aryn exclaimed. "Where did you acquire Laffite's journal?" Looking at him with somewhat disbelief, Anatoly looked down at the journal and stated, "PaPa Vladimir brought me a copy in French last year to inspire me to keep a journal myself, and I have been doing just that."

"Anny, am I in your journal?" Aryn asked, poking at him with her finger.

"Of course you are. But if you call me that one more time you will be a troll in my journal from hereafter."

"Now," said Anatoly firmly as he opened the journal of the pirate. It took Anatoly all the way through lunchtime to explain and make a believer out of Aryn.

"Show me the map, Anny. Sorry, Anatoly." "Alright, look at the pages you put together, each page has a clue for a number to a grid coordinate. Start at the top left to right and read the pages like a book."

Aryn interrupted, "I thought you knew where the treasure is?"

Anatoly said, "I do, but I don't want to write it down for anyone to see until we get it and move it. The clues are riddles, easy"

"So where is the treasure?" Aryn asked

Anatoly stated, "I will show you not tell you, unless you can figure out the riddles."

Aryn looked up from the map and said, "I am still trying to figure you out. How am I supposed to figure out your riddles? That is too hard."

"All you have to do is study a little," Anatoly claimed, as he closed the map and hid it in a box under his bed. "We will go find it when you bring your car."

"Fine Anny, I am going to watch television."

"Fine troll, go rot your brain; I'll be working on my journal."

That evening when MaMa and DaDa got home, Anatoly overheard them talking and learned where PaPa Voss had gone. Together MaMa and DaDa made their dinner and set the table with a candle and some wine. After dinner was finished, they sat talking.

MaMa said, "I set Aryn up in the spare room to stay the night, since your Father has his things in the guest room."

DaDa asked, "Where is the Admiral?"

MaMa stated, "Mara Stacy picked him up this morning in the government car for the briefing at the university."

"Oh yes," said DaDa, "That is why Aryn is staying the evening, because Lt. Stacy is on a mission."

MaMa said, "Don't poke fun. You know, Stacy is all Aryn has in the way of family."

And as if a light came on, DaDa said, "What is Aryn going to do when the lieutenant goes back to the Antarctic with the Admiral?" MaMa moved into the chair next to him, with her wine glass in her left hand, and slipped her right hand behind DaDa's neck and sweetly said, "That is something I wished to talk to you about tonight. What do you think, about Aryn staying with us while her sister is in the Antarctica with your Father?" Without hesitation he looked into her eyes and said, "That would be best for everyone, would it not?" MaMa stood and said, "Then it is settled; I am going to call Mara Stacy right now." "Now?" DaDa said. "Don't worry we have much more to discuss. We will pick up where we left off when I get off the phone."

At the hotel near the University, Admiral Voss and Lieutenant Davis were checked in and finishing dinner when a call came from the front desk for Stacy Davis. Stacy heard the call, and said, "I will take it in the lobby please."

"This is Stacy Davis, how may I help you sir or ma'am?"

"Hey, Stacy. This is Mrs. Voss, I have some good news. We have decided for Aryn to stay with us until you return from Antarctica with the Admiral".

"That is good news Mrs. Voss; that is such a load off my mind. I am so glad you phoned this evening."

"Ok Stacy, we will see you when you return. Tell the Admiral, Anatoly is asking when they will finish the history lesson they began."

"I will surely tell him, Mrs. Voss, thank you again for phoning. Bye Bye".

Stacy returned to the table where she found the Admiral being served coffee. The Admiral looked up and saw Stacy returning. "Are you going to have some coffee?" Stacy motioned to the server for some coffee and said, "Thank you Admiral, I will.

"That was Mrs. Voss on the phone. She called to tell me they invited Aryn to stay with them while we go to Lake Vostok."

The Admiral smiled at the news and said, "Then it is settled; we will be on our way next week. I am anxious to return to my work there."

"She also mentioned Anatoly was asking of a history lesson. You did not mention the Russian mission to the boy, did you, Admiral?"

"Now Lieutenant," Vladimir looked around as if to be looking for spies, "I understand your concern. But the boy keeps everything to himself, and beside that I think he might be a big part of the mission in Russia."

"Admiral!"

"Now look Stacy, no one understands how gifted the boy is. I think in a couple years, with the right prompting, he could be the linguist we have been looking for."

Stacy looked at him in surprise and blurted out, "At five years old"?

"No four and a half. Drink your coffee Lieutenant. In the morning, at the University, you will brief the group of scientist and officers. I want to be observing them to see their reactions to the news, so I can hand pick our team."

"Yes Sir; I think I will go to my room to put everything in order for the morning. Good night Sir".

"Good night Lieutenant."

CHAPTER 3

The Briefing

IN THE MORNING, LIEUTENANT DAVIS had the government car there early. She picked up the Admiral at his room with armed secret service men. The Admiral came to the door in full uniform with all honors, his chest full of medals and ribbons. With briefcases in hand, not a word was spoken by either party; the only sounds were the secret service talking into their headsets. "He's coming out," Stacy heard one say, as they approached the elevator.

Being with the Admiral, Lieutenant Mara Stacy Davis felt so very important and walked a little more erect than usual. The only thing the Admiral said to Lt. Stacy on the way was that when she was ready to introduce him, to give him a few minutes because he would be in an observation room behind the glass. Oh, and to remember the officers could be sent but the scientist's had to volunteer. The Admiral could pull some strings and make them go but He would rather they volunteer.

When they arrived, and the car pulled up out front. Everyone had been directed to their seats and were sitting quietly waiting for the Admiral. Most of them were familiar with the Admiral's work, and they all had heard the conspiracy theories, and discussed them frequently at the school. The Lieutenant was taken a different direction than the Admiral and she was all alone with her thoughts as they walked to the briefing room. As she approached the room, she thought Columbia University seemed an unlikely place for a briefing, but here they were nonetheless. The audience was more scientists than officers but they all had top security clearance, so she could speak freely of the unclassified information and most of the classified. She approached the podium.

"Gentlemen and Ladies," she began speaking softly to immediately gain everyone's undivided attention.

"Most of you are familiar with the HAARP Program, since some of you may have been involved with the designing or application and uses of it. It is the High Frequency Active Auroral Research Program based near Gakona, Alaska. Along with the Orbital Radar mapping combined with surface, seismological measurements have been highly instrumental in our research in the eastern Antarctica, specifically Lake Vostok. This combined effort confirmed that Lake Vostok is under over two miles of solid ice. This is the largest lake discovered in over one hundred years. It is roughly the size of Lake Ontario. But it is much deeper, in some places it is over three thousand feet deep. The water in the lake is still liquid and does not appear to ever have been frozen. Determined by the surface thermal scans, the lake temperature is from 55 to 60 degrees and in different parts of the lake a ten degree variable. We are speculating a subterranean heat source. In addition to this anomaly, the whole lake is covered by a sloping air dome three thousand feet above the surface water, formed from the hot water melting the overlying ice above the lake. We have had delivered a portion of the core samples taken by the Russians in the years before for the examination of your various science departments. We are hoping to propagate interest in the findings of the lake and recruit able bodies for further studies on the site itself."

"Please put your hands down and save any questions for the Admiral and only when he is finished speaking. Then He will give you all a chance for questions.

"The core samples were taken from the bottom of the ice sheets, when they drilled down almost two miles. These core samples have revealed the presence of microbes, nutrients and various gases like methane embedded in the refrozen lake water just above the dome. And as most of you know, such items are typical signatures of biological processes. This completely isolated ecosystem has all the ingredients of an incredible scientific find."

"On the southeast end of Lake Vostok there lies a magnetic anomaly. However, to further study this anomaly would mean we would have to enter this pristine eco-system, exposing or possibly contaminating ,or God forbid, being contaminated. We will take every precaution known to man, but be advised there are risks involved.

With that said, please stand for Admiral Vladimir Voss.

As the Admiral entered the room, there was a hush among the conference. There was nothing but the sound of a few chairs moving slightly. All eyes were on this austere figure who wore his uniform with pride. He walked erectly with definite slow steps…looking everyone in the eye that continued their gaze and did not look away.

Raising the microphone to more suit his height, he began with, "Good morning, I have been observing all of you closely and have had your profiles studied even closer. You were all handpicked for this expedition. In my keen observation, I believe you all to be capable and by now you should know if you are interested. You have to at least admit your curiosity has been peaked."

"I want volunteers to travel with myself and Lieutenant Davis to the Antarctic region to be there when we break through the ice to this unexplored region of our planet. Yes, you will end up in the history books. We will chart unexplored territory and some of you may become famous with your findings. Equally important, we need scientists and officers to stay behind to collect data, supply resources, and to keep in 24-hour contact with the field crews."

"However, the field pay will be almost twice that of the people that stay behind at the university base; which pay will be twice what it is now, since you will be accessible twenty-four/ seven. If anyone is not on board, please stand up turn around and leave right now. Be advised, no one will leave the project after this moment until the project is finished. We will give you another sixty seconds in case someone has to call their Mommy."

Everyone was amused at the statement and looked around at each other then back to the Admiral and waited his next words with quiet ,almost astonished eyes, thinking of what their lives would be like (as much as they could in sixty seconds).

The Admiral looked at his watch, and then with a stern voice exclaimed "GOOD! We have chosen well. Be advised all you have heard today and all our findings henceforth, are classified, top secret information. That means don't tell your Mommies, wives, husbands, best friend, not even your dog. Until this mission is complete and it becomes unclassified, you will discuss it only amongst ourselves. Team, is this fully understood?"

With a rouse of excitement, officers and scientist, young and old, stood to their feet and boldly stated, "Yes sir."

The Admiral came to attention, looked over the crowd of fifty and exclaimed"Welcome to the mission code named,Leviathan."

Then slowly and deliberately, he walked out and returned to the observation room ,watching the crowd with three other dark figures, he met in there earlier.

Lieutenant Davis lowered the microphone back to the lowest setting. "You can sit down. We have much to do. You will be handed a series of papers to be filled out and witnessed oaths taken. Then we will take lunch and return for questions and details."

The Team being regrouped in the large conference room, low muttering and discussions ceased as everyone saw Admiral Voss return to the platform. Lieutenant Stacy handed him some lists as he approached.

"We only lost three people that could not muster the formalities."

"Very well, thank you Lieutenant." The Lieutenant took her seat behind the podium as the Admiral raised the microphone to his liking.

"Ok Team, we only lost three; I don't expect to lose any more, short of death." By now you all have read the briefing and know what is expected of you, whatever field you have chosen, or I should say, whatever field has chosen you. This mission does not involve any other missions in Russia, or Alaska, or in any other part of the world. However, if any news or information is divulged to you, all information will be classified and top secret, until further notice. This does not mean, however, you cannot work on any other mission or job, just that it is classified through the main mission. Any violators will be prosecuted to the full extent of the law under treason, espionage, or any other crime that is applicable, and you will be removed from the project and forbidden to work on any such projects in the future. In layman's terms, your name will be mud. In fact, this mission is directly linked to other missions, and you may be asked to continue your research through another. If you have read the briefings given to you and have a pertinent question that does not pertain to another project but to this project, now is the time to ask."

Hands immediately shot up across the room.

The Admiral started at the front, pointing at a middle-aged small man with dark hair, black rimmed glasses, still wearing his white lab coat. "Stand up and loudly and clearly state your name, rank, m.o.s. or job, and question."

"Thank you sir, Professor Quigg-Dale Quigg professor of Anatomy and Physiology. The longer you are in the Antarctic region, does the magnetic abnormally affect health and well... mental health?" "Thank you Professor. Until now nothing has been documented for either. You will be in charge of this and pick a colleague that is remaining behind here at the university to receive your data and process it through the school's computers for confirmation and comparisons."

"People, when you have more time to thoroughly read the documentation provided, you will better answer these questions amongst yourselves as well as come up with better answers than I have for you. In the meantime, treat the magnetic anomaly like altitude sickness. Drink plenty of water, at least eight glasses a day, and cut down on your caffeine intake. Thank you Professor Quigg; you will give a monthly report on your progress."

"Next question?" Fewer hands were raised this time. "Yes Ma'am in the middle there," pointing with his left index finger straight at a tall woman in uniform at the end of the aisle.

"First Lieutenant Tess Farley, Military Police. Is there security or the need of it at Lake Vostok"?

"Thank you, Lieutenant; when you arrive at the site, report to Captain Dungan for duties. We need more detail in our security; pick someone that is staying behind here to send your reports to. You will be sending data recording to the National Security Agency, and possibly handle further recruitment of security detail."

"Next question?" Two hands remained. "You, in the far rear." A dark man stood from his seat. He was dressed in a black suit and holding a hat in front of him to his chest.

"Thank you, Admiral. My name is Dr. Klingbid, microbiology. Have any of the microorganisms discovered at Lake Vostok been shown to be volatile or detrimental to the health of man, animal or plant life?"

"Dr. Klingbid; I did not know you were here or that you decided to join the Team. It is an honor, sir. The microorganisms sent to Russia that scientists were actually able to culture were different from the microorganisms sent to the United States. Dr. Klingbid, if you could, would you get with me and my assistant? We can hand pick seven people to travel to Russia and the site at Lake Vostok. All data will be available to you and your team, at your discretion, sir. That will be very beneficial for the overall project. And, welcome aboard Dr."

"I see one more hand is that all? Yes ma'am, Miss Bogdan."

"Valerie Bogdan, Literary Writing, Head of the Russian Antarctic Research Institute. Question: Will we be able to report the truth of all events occurring at Lake Vostok, eventually, or will everything remain a mystery forever?"

"Miss Bogdan, I am familiar with your writing abilities, that is why you are on the Team. But facts are all you will be writing, and only after direct approval from me or Lieutenant Davis. Unless you have changed your mind to accompany us to Lake Vostok, all information will be sent to you via email. You will not have clearance to speak to anyone on the project or to access files." The Admiral said this in everyone's hearing so they would know there would be no exceptions.

"If there are no more questions, you can pick up your orders at the door. We will leave next Monday morning. You are dismissed."

The Admiral and Lieutenant left the room together. The car was waiting for them out front to take them back to their hotel. The security followed them back. As they got into the back of the car, the Admiral sat down and let out a long sigh. Then he turned to the Lieutenant and said, "Lieutenant Stacy you are so very proficient and capable; what would I do without you?"

Lieutenant Stacy let down her hair, flipping it back with her fingers, and pretended to boast, "Maybe you can't do without me." She then laughed and said "Thank you, Admiral. It is a joy working with you. I so look forward to the mission."

At that the Admiral smiled and said, "Shall we have dinner this evening?"

Stacy said, "I am so hungry."

The Admiral then replied, "Good, when we arrive, we will get out of these uniforms, and I'll meet you in the dining hall."

Stacy said, "Good, that would be a great end to a good day."

CHAPTER 4

The Treasure & the Promotion

As the Admiral reached his room, there was a call waiting for him. The phone in his room began to ring just as he walked in. It was Anatoly. "Anatoly, what a nice surprise."

"PaPa, when will you be here?"

"Tomorrow afternoon, Anatoly."

"PaPa, we had a mission today, Aryn and I." "But DaDa says I am in trouble. Both of us."

"Anatoly, what could be so bad"?

"PaPa, they said you are part to blame because of the Journal… Lafitte's Journal.

"Oh I see," the Admiral sat down on the bed.

"PaPa, I don't have to give the gold back, do I? Besides, there's no one to give it to. It's mine, right PaPa?"

Admiral Voss laughed out loud, "Anatoly I will see you tomorrow. Do not argue with your parents. I can't wait to hear of your adventure."

"PaPa, I will go write it…in my journal…and then I will send it to you. Both you and Mara Stacy can read about it before you get here

"Splendid idea, grandson. I will see you tomorrow."

"Good night PaPa."

When the Admiral arrived at the dining room, Stacy was already there, at the same table, with the same waiter. After ordering and adjusting his suit, he told Stacy, "I spoke with Anatoly."

Stacy spoke up, anxious to hear, "How are they, Aryn and Anatoly?"

The Admiral cleared his voice, "Seems they had a bit of adventure today. It appears they found some gold and will not speak of where they got it from exactly, but it appears they cannot return it or they have no one to return it to as Anatoly stated."

Stacy put her hands on the table, "Are they okay or are they all right?"

"They are fine, just had a big day that's all, as did we. Stacy, on the plane tomorrow can you bring some of the pertinent paperwork so we might go over it during the flight?" "Yes sir, I certainly will."

The next afternoon as they arrived at the house, Anatoly heard the car door. Any minute Vladimir would be in the yard, halfway up the walk. "PaPa, you are here, you are here and Mara Stacy is with you. Did you read it, did you read it PaPa?"

"I certainly did, it sounds like quite an adventure. Now let's go in and see this map you have drawn."

Aryn met Stacy at the door and hugged her around the waist. "Mara I am glad you are back, let me take your bag. Come on I will show you my room. You can stay with me until you leave with Admiral Voss."

"Ok, Ok, Aryn, slow down, we have the rest of the week and all weekend."

"I know Sis, but we have to move out of the apartment and you have to work and, and"...

"It's okay, Aryn, the Admiral is taking care of all that and I am off work so I am all yours."

"Now come, let's sit on the bed and talk a while."

"Oh yes I know what about, but Mara Stacy it's not my fault,

Anatoly is so smart, he knows so much, I don't know how he does. He says we cannot rest until the mission is complete."

"Aryn, you are the sitter not the other way around."

"I know, but we did not do anything wrong, except worry Mr. and Mrs. Voss. We stayed gone so long because we did so much. Anny said he knew where Jean Lafitte's treasure was and he did, Mara, he really did."

Stacy looked down at her younger sister. "Admiral Voss said he is gifted, and sees things differently, but what did you do with the gold, Aryn?"

"It is Anatoly's gold, he gave me three big pieces for driving and helping him," she told her sister as she reached under her pillow and pulled out three lovely rather large thick coins and placed them in Stacy's hand. "We cleaned them some, but feel how heavy."

Stacy bounced them in the palm of her hand lightly, "They are heavy they must be worth a fortune! How much was there?"

"That is what took so long; there was a whole chest of it. Anatoly gave me three; he had me give a hand full to a man for a boat."

"You bought a boat"!?

"Well Anny says we commandeered it". And Anny kept a great big heavy bag of it for other missions, and then we buried the rest".

"Where did you bury it"?

"Only Anatoly knows, he is making another map, it was just off some sandy beach, somewhere. He knows so much, Stacy."

"So the Admiral ,and now you, keep saying. I think I am starting to believe it."

"I hear Mr. and Mrs. Voss talking to the Admiral. I better go speak with them, are you coming Mara Stacy?"

"No I am going to get cleaned up for dinner Aryn, I will be in directly, and you go on."

As Aryn walked into the room she noticed Anatoly was standing on a bar stool waiving two gold pieces around, telling his story. He was making Aryn out to be a hero of sorts. She blushed as she approached the Vosses."I am sorry if we worried you, we should have called sooner."

"We know Anatoly is in good hands with you Aryn, any way, that is what we get paid for; to worry. Right, MaMa?" Mr. Voss looked over at Mrs. Voss as if to say, "let's don't make a big thing of it."

Then he picked up Anatoly from the stool and put him high in the air and told Anatoly, "Now where is my share of that ill begotten booty son?"

Anatoly giggled and said, "You did not help; you get no gold, Father of mine." Anatoly continued to giggle as DaDa lifted him high in the air and low toward the couch, much like an air plane.

DaDa said, "Then, we must tally the rent and food bills, for you eat your weight in gold," pretending to try and pry the gold from Anatoly's little fingers. "Go and wash up then son," and he whisked him off toward the bath.

Dinner was catered every evening that week, compliments of the Admiral. MaMa called Anatoly to dinner. As he looked around the room, by the doors and against the walls, there seemed to be more secret service than usual. There were a few officers in uniform standing around the table. DaDa was at one end, PaPa at the other end. MaMa was sitting by DaDa then Mara Stacy by PaPa, and Aryn by Stacy Anatoly went straight between Stacy and Aryn, pushing Aryn over, stating, "I am sitting right here," looking up at Mara Stacy for approval.

Stacy reached down, rubbing Anatoly on the top of his head, leaning down a bit said, "That is just where I want you to sit, Anatoly, where I can keep an eye on you." She quickly looked up at Aryn and winked, so Aryn knew she was still close.

The Admiral took the floor, clearing his voice; he told everyone in a stern voice, "Before every one sits down, I have an announcement to make." Just then one of the officers snapped to attention, marched over to the Admiral's side and opened a dark blue velvet box, with ribbons and medals inside.

Turning to Mara with a medal retracted from the box, pinned it on her evening dress. "For exemplary service above and beyond the call of duty, you will receive these awards and meritorious promotion to

Captain. I give you Captain Mara Stacy Davis." Everyone applauded except the officers, who saluted.

Everyone sat down then to eat, as Anatoly was standing in his chair, after climbing up while the Admiral was speaking to get a better view. Anatoly was tugging on Mara Stacy's sleeve, "Can I see?"

Mara leaned down to show Anatoly the medal and opened the dark blue box to show off the insignias to Anatoly. "Maybe one day you can be a Captain."

Anatoly's eyes lit up as he remembered the boat trip the day before then blurted out, "I became a Captain yesterday, of my own boat." Everyone at the table laughed, but only the family knew to what he was referring.

DaDa Voss said, "Anatoly, that story will be better retold at another time."

Aryn chimed in, "Yes, Anatoly some other time, please."

Anatoly hugged Stacy's arm "Congratulations!"

DaDa raised his glass, "Yes congratulations, Captain Davis." Everyone raised their glass.

Quickly finishing dinner, Anatoly snuck off to his room to work on his map. He wanted to finish it before PaPa and Mara Stacy went off on their mission to Antarctica. He must have been working on it for hours because everything got quieter and quieter. Then there was a soft knock at the door, "Anatoly, can I come in"? It was Aryn.

"Entre' vou Madam." Anatoly slanted his speech to make himself sound like someone else.

"Everyone is gone, that is, everyone that is leaving. Do you think you could ask your PaPa if I can sit in on the story when he finishes it?"

Just then PaPa walked in the door . "You certainly can Aryn, since it seems Anatoly has told you of the mission already."

Anatoly kept working on the map as if he didn't hear what was being said. Aryn looked up into Vladimir's warming eyes, a bit nervous, "PaPa--I mean Admiral, I know it is a secret mission, I won't repeat it to any. I would so like to hear you tell it.

"Aryn, you can call me PaPa. You are like family, and your sister and I are going to be working so close, and you will be here with my family. I will be honored to be your PaPa." He put his arm around Aryn's shoulder and gave her a little hug.

"You two get ready for bed and I will be back in to finish the story, u-hum mission." PaPa turned and left the room as silently as he came in.

Stacy saw the Admiral come from the room, and came close to him. Softly she said, "Admiral did I hear you say what I thought I heard I heard you say?"

"Now Stacy, I think they can keep it under their hats."

"They,... they, Aryn knows?" Stacy bruited.

"Apparently Anatoly had memorized the whole first part, and when we left the other day for the university, he recited it to Aryn almost word for word."

"Don't worry, Aryn thinks it is a story."

Stacy stood with her hands on her hips, looking up at the Admiral, to show her disapproval.

"Okay,okay, Captain, when I speak to them, I will emphasize that it is top secret. I will make them both swear an oath under the penalties of espionage or something." This made Stacy smile, a little half smile.

Ready for bed, as PaPa came into the room, Anatoly was just finishing telling Aryn how he can't say a word or interrupt until PaPa was completely finished with the story. "If you wait ,all your questions, well most questions, will be answered right PaPa"?

PaPa tucked Anatoly in and cleared his voice...U-hum. Then started where he left off with the story.

CHAPTER 5

Leviathan Arrives

"The Leviathan was weary. The long journey had taken its toll. Finally the Lead Leviathan started to recognize the passages to the lakes of the Southern region of what we now know as Antarctica, and the South Pole. In his mind, he knew exactly where he wanted to be. The passages to the other lakes were quickly passing him by. Not slowing to consider them or to slow his momentum, heading for the largest lake where the great city of refuge was, he could rest there...still anxious to see the people that had great respect and admiration for him and his great size. His great scales being tempered for the last time were dark red, almost black from the final tempering of this ancient Leviathan's flesh. The great schools of fish from the lake began to appear in front of him and to the sides going around him in swirls from his wake. As they were moving out of his way he thought, "I will herd some of these great fish into the stone traps the men of the city he loved had made and built for Leviathan to catch fish for them all to feast on together. His tail whisking from side to side, separating a number of the larger fish, herding them in the direction of the trap. As he arrived, he herded the fish into the trap as he had done so many times before, closing the underwater gate door with his great tail as the men had designed it. Easily closing, the fish were all caught.

Then the Lead turned, went to the depths of the lake, turned upward, flying out of the water a thousand feet; returning to the surface of the water with a resounding splash; to catch everyone's attention and maybe receive applause and cheering, and hear the ringing of the golden bells. But this great lake was silent. There was no one to surprise; he surfaced his enormous head, and swam for the shore. There was a blue hazy gloom to the place. He looked overhead and then noticed there was no sky.There was an icy ceiling overhead, maybe three thousand feet up or so, there was a great ,light blue ,icy dome over the entire lake, with a reflection of the light of day, dimly illuminating the lake. He blew fire from his nostrils and lit the stone torches that were on the beach. He then plopped his enormous body onto the rocky shore, sharp stones, and sharp pointy things upon the mire under him.

What was so different, what was this, where was everyone? No Leviathan came behind him as of yet. He looked toward the cities habitats; there was no movement--no life at all. No one was working. Things were a wreck; the vessels were upside down against the buildings. He folded his arms, his front legs in front of him and laid his great head upon the shards that felt so good to his tempered skin, and rested.

After a long rest, he was awakened by another great Leviathan bursting through the surface of the water of the lake. Flying upwards barely stopping short of the mark he had set, the dragon turned abruptly to avoid the icy dome ceiling, then turned down striking the dome ceiling with the spikes on the end of his tail, making a thunderous crack. He plunged into the water with the noise of the crash echoing; the sound of the cracking ice reverberating.The dome of the ceiling only cracked a little, as he plunged back into the water, and popped his head out, swimming to shore. The Lead Leviathan awakened, lifted his head, and turned it towards the sound-- looking into the eyes of the second Leviathan; he looking back into Lead's eyes with an expression of wonderment, thinking, what has happened.

The Lead Leviathan laid his head back down, that being the only communication they had or even needed. The second Leviathan pulled himself from the water, and looking about, the only movement was of the great fish splashing about in the trap. But he saw no other movement.

Then leaving the shore toward the city second Leviathan went down the streets, as if looking for someone, someone that always met him, a person of the city that with his family made iron, caps for their teeth, and great claws for battle (leaving the iron shards in their victims). All the people were blacksmiths; all the people were fishermen, and all the people were... gone.

So he lay down in the street with his head at the door of the boy with whom he had great communication with, and rested, right there in the street with his tail and his body laying the length of the street. His body lay against the buildings on both sides of the street. The concrete walls stood three and four stories high. Although his body pressed on both sides, this is where he rested.

When he awoke, the Lead Leviathan had lit all the fires of this ancient city, as if awaiting the return of the people of the realm. But he knew there was no way in except through the caverns, thousands of feet deep under the lake. And under the lake, no man had ever been, even with all the devices they had made to sustain all life.

There were waterfalls from the melting ice running over the tops of the buildings that were attached to the rock walls, and into the side of the mountains. Caves were cut into and through the buildings for mining iron ore and sulfur, gold, salt, and jewels. There was a never-ending resource of minerals for building and ornamentation and weapons of war--though they never had war. No one had ever found the hidden city or the people. Even when they grazed their kine to the coast of the ocean, passer-by ships never stopped or saw their fires. That is…before the city became an icy prison.

Now the waterfalls fell from the edge of the buildings down the streets and into the lake. There was no sign that anyone had been there for days or weeks. No smells of them; no sign at all.

Observing all this, the second Leviathan communicated with Lead Leviathan that other Leviathan were behind him and had taken the passages to the other lakes to rest and to feed.

The great bounty of fish was always there as well. So, Lead Leviathan sent him to the other lakes to bring all Leviathans to the great city of desolation to see the devastation and the tragedy of their prison…to see what they must do. It is a days journey from lake to lake to lake and back again.

They all came in at Lead Leviathan's command. As they were traveling from the other lakes,and through the caverns the rest of Leviathan thought of the communications they had with second Leviathan and what must be hereafter. Nothing would be as they remembered. They would not be catered to and pampered by a city of people who worshiped them. Who would make their iron clad for their claws and their teeth? With whom would they have great feasts? For whom would they catch fish? Who would prepare the places of rest to their liking? Who would mine the sulfur for their desert? Who would build the traps for the fish? Who would milk the fish roe for the hatcheries to supply the overflowing amounts of fish it took to feed Leviathan's veracious appetite? Somehow they must find a way to assume these roles of the men of the city.

They had arms but their claws were too bulky to maneuver such menial tasks that the men did for them. The strength and thickness of their claws were too hard to file down to accommodate tasks completed by such small fingers. They would find a way. Keeping the fires lit was easy. They had mined sulfur for themselves. (When they arrive Lead Leviathan will have answers.

Upon arrival (being foretold by second Leviathan of the height of the dome ceiling), just as it was in the smaller lakes, only higher; they followed second Leviathan in a line. Coming into the lake through the caverns, they sped to the surface one by one, flying through the face of the water. They raised high into the air, turning just before reaching the icy dome ceiling and cracking their massive tail spikes against the light blue icy ceiling. Each Leviathan made a thunderous cracking sound which reverberated and blended echoes with each loud crack before. Crashing into the water's surface with a loud smack, it echoed across the face of the lake and back again. What a site and display of sound! The people of this place would have rang out with great cheering and applause; ringing loudly the golden bells throughout the city. The females would have come to the shores and played harps singing of their greatness. The men would have drummed huge drums resounding to help preserve their muscles for to rest on the rocky shores. But when the echoes diminished, it was silent and hollow sounding like the enclosed pool of water that it is. It was true; no man was left in this place.

As they approached the small group, an assignment was given to each Leviathan. Second Leviathan was sent back through the caverns and chasms to see if there were any openings large enough for Leviathan to pass back to the center of the Earth or just how far they could travel. And only if the Earth had quit its rumbling and quaking.

They let the fish go from the traps. They cooked them in their paths and ate them as they went, whenever they hungered. So the rations began. How long would they be in this ice prison, this place of refuge that turned into an icy prison home?

Second Leviathan returned and told of the dead end he encountered three days journey in. But in his travels, he also encountered great sulfur deposits when great rocks fell away in the passages. This place could not sustain them without the menial tasks of man. They must adapt. Some Leviathan being thousands of years old, understood if they were here thousands of years more, what it would take to sustain them that long. Some scratched and clawed into the Earth for sulfur and carried the sulfur in their claws and in their mouth and filled the great hall of the men with the sulfur they began to mine. This kept them able to temper each other's scales of flesh somewhat, not to the red (almost black) skin of the ancient ones, but to change the green color flesh they were born with to orange and to almost red.

Most jobs were using fire which kept the water temperatures to their liking. Much of the invention of man was still used, such as the gas pipes going deep into the ground; these supplied much fire--an eternal flame of sorts. The torches always lit, and Leviathan lighting his way with his flame that Goeth out of his mouth. Burning lamps out of his mouth, the sparks of fire leap out--by his neesings a light doth shine.

The smaller lakes were used to breed all sorts of fish for food rations. Adapting from the hatcheries of man, oh it was easy with the men that respected them and did not fear them. They might never have that again.

When the plan was finished, the history told daily would include the plan and then they would tell the History of Leviathan thousands of years past to present. It would be part of their daily lives not to forget the young left behind in the North Country. They hoped this catastrophe did not wipe them out or that the men of the North with new technology would not destroy the Earth. They ever encouraged themselves with ancient words of the strength of Leviathan and the ancient stories and how they made it through the Earth maybe for the last time. All this would be told in ancient Russian and their native language together with their prophecy attached, of the future of the boy that would try to make them free, a child that shall lead them. Still now, the prophecy foretold was only partially understood. Nothing else would be communicated but this same thing daily until that day of escape, and then they will add to that history.

It would be forbidden to communicate anything else amongst them or to the new offspring until then. This they communicated daily and did the jobs they were assigned. And their communication was yay and nay only, and this same story only for thousands of years to come. In their stories were included how they adapted (and every Leviathan knew every job), the way they developed the jobs without man and the daily rituals returning from jobs. Daily rituals were developed, as it were, a sport, to prepare for battle, to remain active and strong, to renew their strength. In a line they would go to the depths of the lake, then they all flew to the icy ceilings, cracked their tail spikes against the ceiling (this they did to resemble escape, laughing at the situation, as if they could laugh, and to keep hope); even the ancient ones lead in the exercise. When the offspring were old enough to have the ability, they would attempt to make it to the ceiling. Then they gathered for the stories, the history, the prophecy, the journey, the encouragements of Leviathan and their jobs, first in ancient Russian, then in the Leviathan language. And this, even the youngest of them, could recite together. This they did daily for thousands of years to encourage, and keep to the way that sustains them and practice to keep up their strength and abilities, and this in unison. All young Leviathan knew to recite it. These are all the words they ever heard, all other communications was done with body language. It was all that was necessary. It was all that was allowed. There were no marauders. None strayed, ever.....until.

CHAPTER 6

Illustrations

King James Bible
Job Chapter 41

1 Canst thou draw out leviathan with an hook? or his tongue with a cord which thou lettest down?

2 Canst thou put an hook into his nose? or bore his jaw through with a thorn?

3 Will he make many supplications unto thee? will he speak soft words unto thee?

4 Will he make a covenant with thee? wilt thou take him for a servant for ever?

5 Wilt thou play with him as with a bird? or wilt thou bind him for thy maidens?

6 Shall the companions make a banquet of him? shall they part him among the merchants?

7 Canst thou fill his skin with barbed irons? or his head with fish spears?

8 Lay thine hand upon him, remember the battle, do no more.

9 Behold, the hope of him is in vain: shall not one be cast down even at the sight of him?

10 None is so fierce that dare stir him up: who then is able to stand before me?

11 Who hath prevented me, that I should repay him? whatsoever is under the whole heaven is mine.

12 I will not conceal his parts, nor his power, nor his comely proportion.

13 Who can discover the face of his garment? or who can come to him with his double bridle?

14 Who can open the doors of his face? his teeth are terrible round about.

15 His scales are his pride, shut up together as with a close seal.

16 One is so near to another, that no air can come between them.

17 They are joined one to another, they stick together, that they cannot be sundered.

18 By his neesings a light doth shine, and his eyes are like the eyelids of the morning.

19 Out of his mouth go burning lamps, and sparks of fire leap out.

20 Out of his nostrils goeth smoke, as out of a seething pot or caldron.

21 His breath kindleth coals, and a flame goeth out of his mouth.

22 In his neck remaineth strength, and sorrow is turned into joy before him.

23 The flakes of his flesh are joined together: they are firm in themselves; they cannot be moved.

24 His heart is as firm as a stone; yea, as hard as a piece of the nether millstone.

25 When he raiseth up himself, the mighty are afraid: by reason of breakings they purify themselves.

26 The sword of him that layeth at him cannot hold: the spear, the dart, nor the habergeon.

27 He esteemeth iron as straw, and brass as rotten wood.

28 The arrow cannot make him flee: slingstones are turned with him into stubble.

29 Darts are counted as stubble: he laugheth at the shaking of a spear.

30 Sharp stones are under him: he spreadeth sharp pointed things upon the mire.

31 He maketh the deep to boil like a pot: he maketh the sea like a pot of ointment.

32 He maketh a path to shine after him; one would think the deep to be hoary.

33 Upon Earth there is not his like, who is made without fear.

34 He beholdeth all high things: he is a king over all the children of pride.

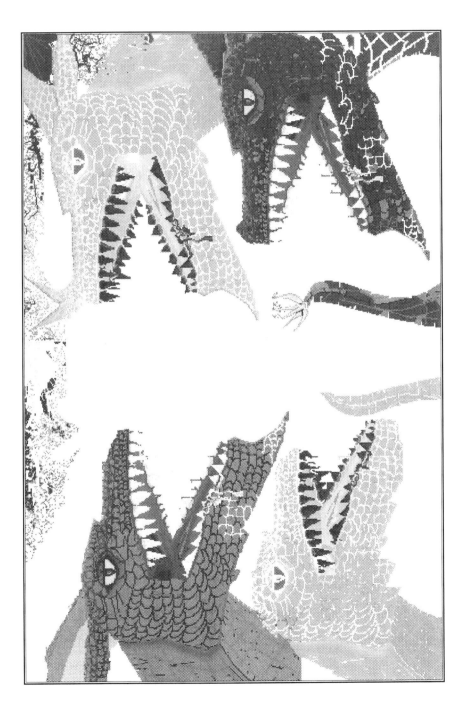

39

CHAPTER 7

Off to the Mission

THE NEXT EVENING ANATOLY CAME to PaPa, "Are you going to finish the story?

PaPa looked down at Anatoly, almost sad, "That is the story Anatoly, and it is finished. The story is on your computer you can listen to it again. It is in the ancient Russian language and also in another unknown language, the ancient language of the Leviathan. Listen to it, and tell me when you start to understand. Work on these languages, Anatoly so I can take you on a mission with me, a mission to Russia."

"Can Aryn go?" Anatoly asked.

"We shall see" PaPa said. "Now, come let's go to your room, and I will show you how to play the tape, and use your translator to assist you." PaPa put his hand on Anatoly's shoulder walking him to his room. He changed his tone, "Have you been practicing your Russian, Anatoly?"

"Oh yes, PaPa, every evening and every day. But DaDa does not have time to speak the language with me; he says it is rude to speak

Russian in front of MaMa. But I have sent you messages on your computer, PaPa. They are all in Russian."

"Good boy, keep working on it. This story has a lot of meaning to it, Anatoly. I cannot tell you of the mission in Russia just yet, but I have a feeling when that day comes, you will be very important to the mission. Now let me show you how we can talk to each other every week, and e/mail every day when we go to the Antarctic."

"PaPa, why can I not go with you? Aryn can go help and..."

Vladimir got serious, "The summers are short, and the winters are harsh. We can only stay a few months, and then we must go to Russia to examine our findings."

"PaPa what is going to happen when you drill through to the lake? Is Leviathan there?"

"Grandson, we don't know what is going to happen. There have been many hypotheses. One is that Lake Vostok will geyser up with great force into the atmosphere and drain the lake"

"Another is that we will discover new microbes or life forms or just something different all together.

And yes, most people do not agree, but Leviathan may be there."

"Can I at least come visit you there?" Anatoly queried.

"Anatoly, you visit me on the computer every day, and I will show you what we are doing. You can learn many things from right at home, and Anatoly, make it part of your home school. You are so advanced, so much more than other children you could make this your only homeschool. Now, let's discuss some other business. How is it you have found Jean Lafitte's treasure when no one else even came close?"

"Well PaPa, when I read his journal I noticed there was a pattern to the pages. But the pages together made a map. He had drawn maps of where he had been, it was really easy. Aryn drove me, we took the metal detector, and the exact grid coordinates were there."

"But Anatoly, why did you move some of the treasure somewhere else?"

"PaPa, in the past, everyone tried to figure out the pirates' treasure map, now they have to figure out my treasure map. You want to see my map, PaPa? Do you?"

"I certainly, do Grandson. I certainly do."

Anatoly pulled the box from under the bed. He took the key that he kept around his neck, and opened his box. Inside there were papers filed, a bag of gold, and miscellaneous personal treasures. He could not lift the box, but barely dragged it out far enough to insert the key. He took the pages of the map and put them together. He told PaPa the riddles, as he showed PapPa the pages.

PaPa looked down with adoration, "You are a smart boy, Anatoly, and I am going to miss you." Then setting his hand on Anatoly's head, he messed up his thick black hair with his fingers.

"PaPa you are going to write every day and call each week, right? And PaPa, don't take so long to come back next time."

"Yes Anatoly, weather permitting."

PaPa, the Admiral, and Mara Stacy, the Captain, said their goodbyes and got in the government vehicle. They were transported to the military base where the plane was waiting. A few of the scientists and officers were already aboard. Awaiting the Admiral and the Captain, the team leaders that were handpicked by the Admiral. These would be the only ones briefed on all the classified documents and were to travel on to the Russian mission. And wherever the mission leads, this team of specialists, each in their own field, would travel ahead or with the Admiral.

It was late in the year and winter. But when they arrived in the Antarctic it would be summer and everything would be thawing. They had much to do before they arrived. The crews had left earlier to prepare the base for the workers that would arrive. Everything had been running all winter with robotics, operating remotely from Russia. The hole in the ice was kept open all winter with the robotic devices spraying thousands of gallons of kerosene on the interior walls of the hole and then being siphoned back to the top to be reloaded for a continual spray. They could drill through in a week's time, but great caution slowed the process. The daily core samples, daily exams, paper work and data entry seemed endless. Everything must be examined closely and inspected thoroughly as not to miss anything abnormal or unusual. All this would help their hypothesis to be more accurate.

It was a long, arduous journey. There was much anticipation on everyone's' part. Fears had to be absolved, and motivation encouraged.

The c1-30s were large enough for the Admiral to hold continuous meetings. This plane was arrayed in such a way that their seats faced inward toward the table set in the middle of what resembled a conference room. Supplies were taken on other planes. Leaders of the teams had many questions. Which hypothesis was more accurate to what really may happen? This was the main topic. The conversation steered toward argument, but the Admiral intervened and spoke softly and lightly of the matter, sometimes joking to lighten the mood. This he did to keep things calm and to train the leaders to do the same with their teams. The Admiral stated that these things must be done to calm any fears, and to keep order so people could act in a crises, and not react with emotion. All hypotheses were welcome, all facts were welcome, but arguments and fears will be dissolved instantly.

Everyone was well versed on how they should respond to their subordinates, who were, as the Admiral put it, "equal on this expedition, but on a need to know basis."

"I want to keep the dangers to an absolute minimum." As the Admiral began to speak, everyone hushed. "We need a response for each hypothesis. We need a team to take action in case of problems. Everyone should know each others' job; each person should know each other's response to every possible danger, and action for each reaction. We have taken every precaution, equipment for every possible mishap. Decompression chambers are available in the event we can enter through the dome to the depths of the lake. We don't know the pressure even under the ice. A lot of years of preparation have gone into this operation. All the equipment we need is down there, ready to be used. All of you men and women have been hand selected, with all of your attributes, imperfections, and knowledge taken into consideration. You will find in your quarter's things to your liking, things you are accustom to. We want you to be as comfortable as possible. We need your minds to be sharp. We need your responses to be accurate, and we need your timing to be acute. We need to plan as if this expedition could change the world, as we know it. And it very well may do just that. We don't know what we are going to find. "Are there any questions?"

Dr klingbid spoke up. "Admiral Voss, what about the medical facility?"

The Admiral looked to Captain Davis,"Captain Davis."

Captain Davis picked up her notebook and spoke up, "We have been building one of the best field hospitals possible, of its kind, with instruments for every scenario. It is small, but we have everything we need for case-by-case treatment. We have a burn unit, medical scans, M.R.I., C.A.T scans, ultra sound, and a barrage of x-ray machines. There are two operating rooms with complete surgical staff and equipment to accommodate them; all with the latest technology. All of this is at your disposal for doctors and scientists alike. Upon arrival, everyone will be checked out thoroughly for any pre-existing conditions they may have and daily noting any changes in anyone's appearance or metaphysical outlook."

The Admiral pulled back to the microphone, "Thank you Lieutenant, and excuse me;... Captain Davis."

One of the officers in the team standing around the table, let out a whoop, followed by a few more, a sort of congratulatory yell for the Captain becoming captain.

The team became quiet when the Admiral cleared his voice. "Are there any more questions? Lieutenant Griner."

"Yes sir, the magnetic anomaly; what is your personal opinion as to what it is?"

The Admiral sat erect in his seat, "It has been said that it is possible that an ancient city exists, below the ice. And that is also my belief. There is something that has survived there. The temperature of Lake Vostok seems to be intentional or you might say the temperature makes it habitable. And no, this is not the X

Files. I do not believe in aliens, though the peoples or creatures of the lake may be alien to us. We are drilling over the deepest part of the lake. And we hope to send down unmanned vessels into the waters to send back signals, sound and video, to which we will all be recording and logging reports. We will not send down any personnel for fear of exposing or being exposed to the unknown of this pristine environment. We will all be monitoring data until such a time it is deemed safe to go down. And then only volunteers, in good physical condition will go on such an expedition. Any further questions? Yes, Doctor Klingbid."

"The Russian mission." The Doctor stood, and then began again. "The Russian mission, that follows this one; how is it connected? And this team that is on the plane, will they be able to help pick the team to go on to this mission?"

The Admiral sighed with a deep sigh, "Doctor Klingbid, I guess it is time to reveal the Russian mission, since most of this team will be going directly there from the Antarctic. And yes, after closely monitoring the staff helping on this, we will need your input, or rather daily reports of possible candidates to go on to Russia."

"You are probably wondering why we brought a linguist, or should I say a specialist in language on this mission. We have discovered something that is now at the Russian base, secured with chains in an underground steel vault. And we have been recording the languages. I know... I understand it sounds like a fairy tale. But we have found a Leviathan; or what we believe to be a small one.

"On our last mission to the Antarctic, there was a crack in the ice. After discovering warm air coming from inside the ice, a five man expedition team explored the depths of the ice. Two men returned and later died of unknown causes. The other three went deep into the chasm, and slid to the bottom. Two men disappeared, and a woman that was injured does not seem to remember what happened inside. She was brought out by this Leviathan. Its fierce countenance caused panic and fear. Though the woman kept insisting it would not harm us. At that time, the Leviathan was smaller and could fit out through the crevice, just before the ice closed behind the Leviathan because of the extreme temperatures. Then the Leviathan could not return from which it came. When the woman spoke, all she could say was the creature is friendly, not to hurt it. And that it saved her. We captured that Leviathan, using the robotics' on the site, and using chains; chains larger than ship's chains is what it took to hold the Leviathan. We have recorded the whole event, from the capture to the captivity."

Every evening, like clockwork, the Leviathan recites a story of sorts. First, in a more Ancient Russian, then in an unknown language, it recites what is possibly the same story. We believe and have named the language the Leviathan language; but no one has been able to interpret, decipher, or understand it. But the ancient Russian language has been interpreted to the best of our several abilities. And I will now play for you with a full video the Leviathan telling the story in Russian with the translation in English at the bottom of the screen. If you care to continue, watch the Leviathan language as well, with the same words as before in English. As I said before, we don't know if he or she is telling the same story or not. But this mission to Russia and what was said in this plane will not be repeated outside this plane until we arrive in Russia and can see for ourselves."

Just then almost everyone on the plane had a question, raising their hand, or standing to their feet. All the Admiral would say is, "Let us watch the tape, and I want to emphasize again to you all to keep this to yourselves. Do not discuss it out loud after this trip until we arrive in Russia, then all your questions will be answered. Then we will see firsthand, what the Leviathan eats, or rather what we have been feeding it; mostly fish, to which you will see on this tape how he cooks the fish with the breath of his nostrils or mouth or however it generates or manipulates the flame. But it seems the flame of fire is not as strong as it once was, but we feel maybe we ought to keep it that way not knowing its capabilities. And as I said before, we believe it to be maybe the smallest of this creature."

The Admiral started the tape. On the screen, the fierce creature made some to gasp; one fainted at the sight and thought of the existence of this unknown reality. How could this be? Why have none heard of this before? This seemed to change the whole expedition.

The Admiral firmly stated as he stood, "No more questions, no more conversations, watch this as many times as you like." Then the Admiral turned and went to the front of the plane. Most everyone responded by doing just that and was transfixed toward the screen.

Everyone's eyes were widened as they saw this creature manipulate words. Everyone's attention was toward the screen affixed with astonishment, some mouths dropped open, some couldn't read the words the first time, unable to take their eyes from the visage of the majestic creature.

CHAPTER 8

The Escape

THE PLANE ARRIVED, AND IT was a sunny day. The team leaders disembarked the plane, and they were all kind of stoic. Some were met by some of their team, and they noticed a definite difference in the team leaders, and wondered what had transpired on the plane. Nevertheless, as the Admiral commanded, none spoke of the mission, and turned to their duties, and to explore this new environment that would be their home for several months.

There was a bit of tension in the air, but that soon expired with the long hours and days of work. The first team meeting was called by the Admiral, after they had arrived, checked into their quarters, and each person had a complete medical checkup. All their teams had already been there, checked in, and all were anxious to get started. The Captain called the first meeting to order.

Then Admiral Voss entered the room, and his very presence commanded respect, everyone was silent.

Clearing his voice, he began, "We can begin drilling immediately, every ten feet we will stop, take new core samples, check for changes in the environment around us, and don't forget to report in for medical examinations at the end of every day."

"The samples will be tested, split, and a portion sent to the university, and a portion sent to the Russian center for further testing and comparison by our teams left at home to assure our observations are accurate and precise."

"At ten feet a day it will give us time to monitor and check all systems, research new scientific facts and findings. And we will approach the dome ceiling in a timely fashion so we will be prepared for almost any scenario. Everyone to your stations, everyone stay calm and keep order; everyone stay with your teams. Let's get busy; we have a mission to complete and a job to do, and people...let's have fun. Meeting is adjourned."

Everyone was excited and reported to their post. The first drilling began. A hundred yards left to drill, ten feet a day. You could see people doing the math, the drilling stopped as fast as it started. The sprayers continually siphoned the kerosene from the bottom and sprayed the walls of the hole, so no ground would be lost. Then as it got quiet, the people that just arrived heard for the first time what seemed to be a muttered low rumbling crack of the ice. It was more of a systematic deliberate crack. Crack. Crack. Over and over.

Some people that had been there a while, seemed to be counting the steady consecutive drum-like echoing sound coming from the hole. The Admiral's voice came over the intercom, "People quit standing around; we have things to do and places to be. The following people report to the clinic for medical exams and do so every day at this same time." Captain Davis took the microphone in hand and almost drowning out the drum-like sound, read a list of names and times to report to the clinic.

Then after what seemed an eternity, the drumming sound stopped. Everyone was afraid to speculate as to what the sound was, and some kept repeating it is only the ice cracking from the drilling.

Daily finishing their ten feet, no matter what time they finished, at the same time every day the reverberating, cracking began and stopped at the same time. At the daily team meeting, the cracking drumbeat was addressed. What could it mean?

The core drill samples were much the same every day.

Some days the chemical components varied, but no new detectable samples. The closer they got, the reverberations seemed louder, and finally they stopped. It was much the same every day.

One member when he went for his medical exam, could not stop shaking and went into hysterics. The fear of the unknown drove him to almost certain madness, and he stayed at the medical facility. Another handled samples without all the protective clothing; protocol was not observed to the letter. The man was treated for chemical burns. He was to be closely monitored and observed, putting salve on his arms. Security of protocol was enhanced so this would not happen again.

Every day meant ten more feet. Like clockwork. Everyone worked with anticipation, counting the feet together. At the team leader meeting being held, the Admiral stated the obvious; every person knew there was thirty feet left.

"Three days from now we will make history. Lake Vostok, the new discovery. Whatever we may find, our records are perfect, waiting to break through to this pristine environment in three days. We have some equipment repair so we will begin a little late today. So it will be a good time to double check your stations and encourage your teams."

"Admiral Voss," a small man in a white lab coat spoke up. "Team leader Sands sir, Eric Sands."

The Admiral hesitated to call on the man, not knowing what he might bring up, but then relenting, thinking; he is a diligent man, address him. "Yes, Eric Sands, speak up man."

Almost choking on his words Eric began, "Well sir, maybe we should skip a day, starting late we may still be drilling when the cracking sound starts."

"Son," the Admiral solemnly addressed him, "You know what time it starts, and stops, you can still do your counting." The Admiral stood, turning his head halfway about as he exited the room, he barked out, "To your post people."

It was kind of a break from the normal routine; people had time for an extra cup of coffee, and small talk.

Then the Captain's voice came over the intercom, "Man your posts, the repairs are made, the drilling will resume." The drills began slowly turning, once at normal speed some began counting the feet, down from ten, time past, nine, checking all systems. Slowly time passed, and the noisy motors steady turning was loud but almost soothing, becoming accustomed to the daily task. Slowly the massive drill descended, almost two miles beneath the ice. Most everyone was counting now, if not aloud then under their breath, seven, the cameras in the hole were being closely monitored; all personnel was inside during the drilling. The robotics were completely remote controlled from the massive control panel; each person knew their job. Each systems checks were announced minute by minute, six. Eric Sands was watching his watch and then announced nervously, "It's time for the cracking to start!" Some were a little distracted by this announcement and jumped the controls they had been so steady on.

Just then someone asked, "Should we shut the drill down?" someone else announced louder, "Shut the drills down?"

"Negative," the Admiral barked, but it was too late, some shut down while others resumed the controls. The drill was thrown into a kind of kilter. Reports were coming from all over; "Something is wrong, the cracking is affecting the drill."

"Stop all operations, lower the siphoning hoses; get that kerosene out," the Admiral shouted. "Everyone man your post and stay calm; this is just another day."

The drills slowed and finally stopped, the siphoning pumps began to draw all the kerosene to the top and into the tanks, "Ready to start the spraying sir."

"Belay that, do not start the spraying," the Admiral commanded.

Then for a moment everything was quiet, except for the steady all-too-familiar cracking sound. Some had forgotten it was that time already since they had started late.

"Check all the cameras; make sure this is being recorded. Captain Davis, get the Russian center on the phone." Admiral Voss was handing out commands loud enough for everyone's hearing.

The thunderous cracking continued, reverberating in everyone's ears--something was different. Just then a thunderous quaking shook the buildings and the heavy drills, motors, and pumps that were fastened to the ice. All began to collapse into the hole ,ice exploding. Everyone gasped. "It is breaking through on its own, Admiral, what do we do?"

"Monitor, just monitor," the Admiral remanded.

People seemed to forget their jobs. Some began to panic. Just as everything began to fall into the hole, the great hole was filled with water, ice and debris instantly filling then gushing out. Geysering into the air with all the equipment. Then as it were great buildings passing by the monitors up and out of the hole, massive bodies out into the atmosphere. All the waters and ice with it flying, pushing forth and out and up. Some debris fell into the snow, some hit the roof and walls of the buildings. The massive red bodies passing by together with the water and ice forced its way up and out of the sight of the cameras. Thunderous crashing kept pounding the site.

Everyone stood astonished, transfixed on the screens before them. "What was that?" some together exclaimed. Again and again as quickly as it started the sky became black and great amounts of water began falling outside. Could they shut it off? Two miles of ice began to collapse. The hole grew ever larger.

The Admiral barked out commands, "Everyone in the buildings, closest to the hole, leave your post and retreat to the further most buildings."

"Admiral, we have a lot of it on tape," one exclaimed. The water began to stop geysering from the hole after what seemed like an eternity. The Admiral called a team leader meeting.

"Team leaders to the conference room. transfer the recordings to the conference room and the rest of the team stay at your post, and report any further activity directly to me." He then turned and left the room, the team leaders followed.

The tapes were reviewed in the conference room. The team leaders all knew what it was that came out of the ice but none spoke of it. There would be time on the Russian mission to discuss everything in detail.

The Admiral began to address the team leaders. "Well it happened kind of abruptly, but the first part of the mission is finished. No one goes outside until further notice. Use the robotics to capture samples for analysis. Also use the robotics to begin to rebuild over the hole so we can begin our decent as soon as possible into the depths of the lake, whatever may be left of it," he chuckled with a half grin.

Everyone was so used to starting their duties the same way, but without the drilling and the monitoring, no one knew what to do. The drilling was over. They awaited the Admiral's orders. The Admiral called another team leader meeting. "Team leaders, keep your team calm. We are now in Phase II of the mission. The worst should be behind us. What happened yesterday is out of our hands. What happens tomorrow is up to us. We must continue the mission. Get your teams together for a meeting. We will all meet in the cafeteria and congratulate our teams on a job well done and begin Phase II of the operation...exploration of Lake Vostok. We have monitored all that happened yesterday. We will forget it. It is out of our hands. The Russian government has taken over that part of our operation. The robotic exploration of Lake Vostok is our main concern. We will further discuss what happened yesterday when we arrive in Russia and we know more. You are dismissed to the cafeteria. Have a good breakfast and we will have a good day."

Everyone left the room. The team leaders were in good spirits. The teams had questions. The team leaders were fully trained in not answering the questions but directing their teams to the next phase of the mission. Everyone met in the cafeteria, there was a low roar of voices .Teams congratulating one another.

The Admiral came in with Captain Davis and called the meeting to order. He stood, tapped the microphone set up for him, and with his usual stern voice said, "Congratulations everyone. Congratulations teams on a job well done on Phase I. We begin Phase II immediately.

The tests came back. Nothing is any different than it was before. We now have access to the hole. Kerosene sprayers are being reset and new equipment installed. We must begin to prepare the robotics to descend into Lake Vostok and begin sampling. Anyone wishing to volunteer, when the tests are complete, may go on the expedition. We will monitor through three robots. One will be suspended from the dome's icy ceiling for complete observation for any signs of life. The second will be dropped onto Lake Vostok. The third will go into the depths of the Lake to see how far we can descend into this nearly 3,500 foot deep lake. Your jobs will change. Everyone will monitor and report and record all that is seen. We will have at least one more day of staying inside. No one will go outside until further notice. All will be done by complete robotics until further notice. If that relinquishes you of your job, get with your team leader for a new assignment until the robotics phase is finalized. Again, congratulations to each and every one of you on a job well done. Report to your teams back home, and congratulate them. Enjoy your breakfast."

CHAPTER 9

Leviathan Awaits

THE DAILY MUNDANE EVENTS, THE uneventful happenings of the Leviathan nation, day in and day out, year in and year out, this prison where Leviathan had learned to live; the work was every day the same. Their actions were still the same. Their jobs never changed. Mining for sulfur. At their return, they compelled themselves with great force out of the Lake to the icy ceiling crashing their tails with a thunderous crash against the dome ceiling. Everyone made their mark close to the same spot in the dome, to resemble their escape. To be free once more. To be able to tell a new story instead of the history they recited every day. First in the Ancient Russian language they knew not,except of the story of the Leviathan, recited to them when they were young, that all of them could repeat; though something changed the year before.

The radar monitoring was felt by the Leviathan. Behind the building above the caves, a fissure opened up and three men, one the female type, came in through the crack and slid into their environment. The female was hurt. Without hesitation, the smallest of the Leviathan returned her to the surface. Clawing with its great legs, crawling up the icy wall through the fissure. It could barely fit through. Clutching the female in her front left paw, The Leviathan clawed its way to the top wasting no time. Man could save her. Not knowing the fissure would close behind this Leviathan that had this noble act in mind. The other Leviathan waited for the small Leviathan's return. When the ice closed, they realize she would not return. The two men were in good health. Upon site of the Leviathan the two men cowered into a corner of a building for refuge where the Leviathan could not reach them. Why did they take their friend from this expedition? Where did they take her? They had many questions. Then in the evening, under the light of the torches on the beach , on the shore of the lake, they heard someone speaking in Russian and they listened. It was almost archaic Russian. They didn't understand.

As they approached the windows and doors of the city that they found themselves in, there was cooked fish, a pile of cooked fish, sitting at the door. A stream of water came through the roof and ran out of the building into the street; it seemed to be fresh. They had tests kits in their backpacks. They tested the water and were happy to see it was drinkable. But where did the fish come from? How did these great creatures know that they needed food? They tested the fish and ate some and sneaked down the street to try to get a better hearing of the story being told in the Russian language. They could make out bits and pieces. The two Russians that were left were stranded in this under world city. They were being kept alive and ignored, almost as if it didn't matter that they were there.

They listened to the story. It was the story of Leviathan. Days passed and they ventured out (when most of the Leviathan were out sustaining themselves) through the doors that opened out into the city. What kind of civilization was there? There was only this creature. They found signs of man having been there. They spoke to each other of what this meant, what they must do, how they could return.

Just then a great Leviathan plopped himself onto the rocky shore of the lake, laid down, pointing his head straight toward them. It was a thunderous event; he crashed his head down to the ground and looked with his steely, fiery eyes straight at the two men. Their first impulse was to run; instead, they stood frozen. One of the men's knees began to knock in fear and smote together.

It was an ancient Leviathan and he spoke in the ancient language. He realized that the men did not understand him. He then recited some of the story in Russian and the men understood the language. Leviathan never communicated in this language before and wasn't sure how it was done. Now he understood why they learned Russian this whole time. But all he knew was the story and history told in Russian. Just then the other Leviathan returned from work and their labors and with a quaking reverberating splash, came through the water's surface. They flew toward the ceiling, and turning down they crashed their tails on the ceiling, all in a line. The men hid themselves in the building. They were close, so close, they meant no harm. When the rest of the Leviathan finished their ritual of cracking the ceiling, they came and lay on the shore. The ancient one stood high upon his back legs and began the history of the great Leviathan in ancient Russian first, then in their own language. The men could only make out parts of the story, but they seemed to start to understand what was going on. The Leviathan meant no harm. All Leviathans' eyes were on the men instead of the great ancestor. But they listened intently as they watched the men's reactions. The men were still unsure of the Leviathan's intentions. They sat every night and listened, relearning their own language as it was in the old days; They remembered what their grandparents taught them of their language that changed so much over the years.

The smallest of the Leviathan brought them fish and cooked them. All the older Leviathan knew the men could help them, and it seemed to the men that they were sort of "pets" of the Leviathan, and they were certainly at their mercy... this giant of creatures, with terrible sharp teeth roundabout and their scales so closely knit together, air could not pass through. They observed them and ate the food that was provided for them. The men wandered through the building the Leviathan could not get into. They found the store of treasure that was left by a civilization long gone. They didn't venture through the mine shafts of the buildings. They started to light torches that hadn't been lit since the last humans were there. Some Leviathan were trying to do the blacksmith's job but their figures were too large and their claws too long for most of the tasks.

The Russians' names were only important to each other. Leviathan didn't care to introduce themselves. They didn't care to communicate other than the communication of the story of history; it is almost as if they ignored them. They always watched them as the stories came every evening. Time dragged on.

These two men looked to assume roles. They greedily found their way into the mines and mined jewels and coal, but to what avail? They could not use them. If they ever escaped, they knew of the mission to drill through the ice that they began with their teams. They knew the Admiral would return for them eventually, if they could sustain life. It was easy to sustain life there with the Leviathan's help. The fish gates were open. The Russians understood that they could operate hatcheries, and it excited them that they could return the favor to Leviathan. Once again they could open the city's hatcheries and perform the work of the blacksmiths. It was evident that someone had made great iron claws and caps for the teeth of the Leviathan. The Leviathan had forgotten why they didn't have any need of this here. There were no battles, only sustaining life and doing the mundane labor. The two Russians turned to these jobs and began to work. What an exciting life to work side by side with this enormous creature! Though communication was simple, it was exciting. The most behemoth of this creature still struck fear in their hearts just by his enormous size and strength. They came close to the smallest of the Leviathan, and they readily examined each other every evening. Closer and closer they came. The fears subsided. The days pressed on and they fell into the routine of the Leviathan.

Then the day came that they heard in the icy dome ceiling above their home, noises echoing through their chambers; unknown and unfamiliar noises ever drawing closer. The Russians understood that the Admiral was back. He was drilling.

One day the greatest of the Leviathan didn't leave the shores. He sat waiting for men to come out of the buildings. When the two men came out, they saw the Leviathan still lying on the shore. The most behemoth of the Leviathan, he communicated with his eyes looking at the men, looking at the dome ceiling, and then looking back at the men. As if to say, you know what this is, tell me. The men tried to explain. The Russian language had changed so much. The Leviathan, with an empty look in his eyes, turned his head away from them breathing fire which leaped from his nostrils and bounced against the stony wall of the building, as if to say "communicate with your people, we have the power to protect ourselves" and then recited part of the story. The men knew that they understood that the men of the North Country once again would be in fear of them and try to hurt them. The two Russians explained, "We will talk to them, we will explain to them. We will let them know that Leviathan means no harm." The Leviathan just shook his head and closed his eyes. All of them knew what the outcome would be. They would not see them as these two Russians saw them. In their haste, they would be angry. The ancient Leviathan turned, dove into the waters, and went into the depths.

All the Leviathan returned to that same shore every evening at the same time and performed their rituals. Some returned to other lakes, soon returning to this great Lake Vostok to rest. They communicated to each other that the day of escape was coming. They aimed their tails to the place of the noise of the drilling coming from above, not knowing man's devices, not understanding how it was they were breaking through the ice when these behemoth creatures could not break through, no matter what they did. Understanding they must retrieve the smallest of the Leviathan that left and could not return. Understanding they must return to the Barents Sea to see if any of the ancient Leviathan that was left were still there. They must return. They must find the young Leviathan that was to be their Queen. She was the smallest but they understood that she had compassion on the female of the men that joined their society. They understood that she could not return, so they made a plan. The Russian drew pictures of the base and drill rigs and mapped what they remembered of the Antarctic.

The Leviathan communicated with the Russians that they would be able to break free from this icy prison and when the pressures of the chamber of the dome of the Lake released, they would have to be there to fly out, not knowing what they would be flying out into. The drilling came ever closer. The cracking became ever more hollow sounding. The Leviathan knew they were getting closer and closer to the day, and they hatched a plan; follow us, we know the way…once we escape, the waters may have changed some.

They knew the way through the seas. The little Leviathan that were born there would have to follow; they did not know the way to the home of the North. But until that day, they kept up their duties. They did as the Leviathan always had done, they cracked the ceiling every evening.

This day was different. As they began to crack the ceiling with the spikes on their massive tails, today the ice was giving way. Instead of returning to the shores for their stories, they went in a circle in the depths of the water and returned to the line, cracking the ceiling one after another. Then the ceiling began to fall into the water with great splashes and the Leviathan made a line, just as they had done every day. Instead of stopping at the ceiling, they burst through the pressures escaping through the hole in the ceiling. They helped push up through the hole in the icy dome

This was the day all that were in the lake escaped. Some at the other lakes were to stay behind in the hopes of everyone returning if there was a way to keep the ice ceiling open. They would return for the ones who maintained the city that they once loved. The only city that some of them knew. The city they called home. They would all return one day.

As they came in through the caverns and chasms that evening, the great elder was gone. The two men were left. They looked to the men and they recited the story and history as if they were all there. The men recited it with them in Russian, but the Leviathan language they could not speak or understand. It was too hard to learn. The Leviathan that remained, sustained the men and the men sustained the Leviathan. All Leviathan who escaped were clad with iron on their teeth and claws ready for battle. They escaped through the hole in the icy ceiling dome, flying through the atmosphere. They plunged into the deepest ocean surrounding what was once their icy prison home; they plunged into the ocean, free at last. The cold waters tempered their scales; turning their scales into a light blue color. The young Leviathan needed to find the fires that tempered the ancestors' scales, so one day, they too, could be red and black with tempering of the great gianormous ancestors.

The icy waters not affecting them, they went down into the depths of the ocean, remembering the sights, lighting the way as they went with the flame of their nostrils. Following in their wake, the smaller Leviathan were drawn along as they did in the caverns and chasms of their home, but they were free. They saw sights they never saw before. The giant Leviathan remembered the sights and the activity of the ocean depths. They stopped and ate of the foods they had not eaten of in so many years. It was changed. The young Leviathan were almost excited, if they could be excited, at this change.

They were a burst of energy streaming through this ocean current day and night, ever heading North, not knowing that sometimes passing ships were rating them on their instruments, but they did not care for man's devices. They had a mission of their own: return to the North and find Leviathan alive. Find the offspring they left, now to be thousands of years old themselves, if they survived man's devices. Some of the communications they had in stories should be foretold by the Leviathan of the North, but of the icy prison, Leviathan of the North would know nothing of.

They feasted on whatever they wanted. A great whale crossed their path, and the Leviathan, like a pack of wolves, attacked and consumed the whale. Sharks were no match for Leviathan. It was like the polar bears of old times, just a morsel. They were going to change the world, the world they didn't even know of. Man would ever more see them as the beast rising from the sea. Leviathan would be once more hated for their fierce appearance. The old animosity would be stricken into their stony hearts once again. They must avoid man at every cost. Though they had great size, they were the stealthiest of all the creatures. Though they were enormous, the depths of the oceans were great, and they could hide. So they headed North.

CHAPTER 10

The Vosses Ready for Russia

ANATOLY, WITH THE HELP OF Aryn, planned a boat trip to show MaMa and DaDa Voss how they found the treasure. Anatoly said, "I'm the captain, DaDa."

DaDa Voss said, "Anything you say, captain, is fine with me." Anatoly had a great day with Aryn and MaMa and DaDa. DaDa found someone to buy the boat, so that they had a captain for the day to drive the boat. It didn't matter if anyone knew where the treasure was because the treasure was moved. They saw dolphins and manarays jumping out of the water. It was a great day at the beach. Anatoly told MaMa, "We must return home. PaPa is going to call me tonight. Tonight's the night; he's been emailing me."

So MaMa said, "Give the orders." He stood up on the deck and hollered in a loud voice, "Turn the boat about; we are heading home."

They cut the time close, so Anatoly ran directly to his room when they returned home. Aryn was helping to carry things in and was talking to MaMa Voss. "Mrs. Voss, being with Anatoly is such a pleasure. It's like being with a little adult. He's so smart."

MaMa looked down at Aryn and said, "You're smart too, Aryn."

"Yeah, but Mrs. Voss, he's like genius or something smart."

"Yes, he is that, Aryn. We want to thank you for taking such good care of Anatoly while we are working. It means so much to his Father and I."

"That's okay, Mrs. Voss. I love being with Anatoly. I learn so much. He makes home school easy. He teaches me more than I teach him, but I would never tell him that."

Mrs. Voss looked down and smiled, putting her hand on Aryn's shoulder and said, "Let's get cleaned up for dinner."

Anatoly ran to his room, turned on his computer that PaPa gave him, and counted down the minutes. He looked over some notes from the ancient German he was learning. Just then, PaPa came on.

"Anatoly, how's my favorite grandson?"

Anatoly looked into the computer and got close and said, "PaPa, I'm your ONLY grandson."

PaPa said, "Oh yes, that's right. How's my only grandson?"

"Fine, PaPa, DaDa sold the boat.....and the new boat captain took us out, and I took them where I found the treasure but I'm not showing them where I hid it."

"That's fine."

"PaPa, I waited to see you before I asked you. Who is on the tape? The voice on the tape? The voice is not yours, and I'm used to you telling me stories. Who is on the tape?"

PaPa smiled out of the corner of his mouth and asked, "Anatoly, have you been learning anything?"

"Oh yes.......I don't understand all the words; I can't find them on the computer of the ancient Russian, but the other language sounds backwards."

"Oh?" PaPa exclaimed.

"It's familiar, PaPa, it's familiar language and the Russian is almost the same. The words are at the bottom of the screen but there is no picture. Who is talking, PaPa?"

"Anatoly, when you are ready and you understand more, we will talk about who's talking. You can hear his voice. Can you make out his words?"

"I'm working on it, PaPa, everyday. Sometimes at night, when I can't sleep, I work on it. PaPa, can I come to Russia when you go to Russia?"

"Anatoly, maybe next year, not this year."

"PaPa, I'll pay my own way to come, I'll pay with the gold if I can come."

"That's right, Anatoly, when you are ready, after you learn the language."

"But PaPa…."

CHAPTER 11

Dragon

CORRESPONDENCE BETWEEN ANATOLY AND PAPA continued day after day, each of them forming a journal. The events of the day unfolded day by day; both had bad and good days. Each day was a new learning experience. All recorded and documented. All to further their advancement, to retain the knowledge, all in the name of a mission.

From one mission to another, PaPa, the Admiral, wanted Anatoly to reach his full potential with little setbacks. Anatoly was so brilliantly gifted and he never doubted he was the one that would be able to interpret and decode the Leviathan language. Captain Stacy who worked side-by-side by Vladimir Voss, the Admiral, didn't know what his plans were. She was on a need-to-know basis as everyone else, for their daily mundane tasks. All the events at Lake Vostok were recorded in the Admiral's journals. But the Admiral held back some of his journals from Anatoly for a future date.

Aryn tried to limit the adventures for safety's sake but Anatoly was busy anyway interpreting language, trying to get Aryn interested, but everyone has their own agenda. One day when the Vosses came home Aryn met them at the door. "Oh, I am so glad to see you Mr. and Mrs. Voss. I am worried about Anatoly."

"Why Aryn; what is it?"

"He has been outside all day just staring motionless, frozen."

"Did something happen today, Aryn?" Mrs. Voss inquired.

"Well, I was doing my school work on the living room computer, and Anatoly was in his room like always, and I went in to ask him if he wanted some lunch. He went into a fit, throwing himself on the floor. I did like you said Mrs. Voss, carried him to the back yard. When he sat in his special chair, he froze like that," she pointed out the back window.

Anatoly still sitting in the chair, was watching the birds and animals they fed daily in the garden.

"He looks fine to me, Aryn," Father retorted.

"But I'm worried. He hasn't eaten all day and I haven't seen him move. Once, when I was watching him, a bird even landed on him."

Mr. and Mrs. Voss said, "Well, let's go see." They slowly opened the door and retreated into the backyard, talking amongst themselves. As they approached Anatoly, they noticed some birds took off from around him, and a squirrel scampered up the tree. There sat Anatoly in his chair frozen, just as Aryn said.

Father approached him and touched him on his arm. "Is everything okay, Anatoly?"

Without looking up or moving, Anatoly stated, "Yes Father, everything is okay, except, I was learning the bird's language and they were talking to me. I was feeding them here, and well, I think you scared them away."

Mrs. Voss leaned down and stroked his hair. She said "Anatoly, do you want to come in and eat? I brought your favorite."

Anatoly, still looking straight forward, calmly and quietly said, "Yes, Mother, I am hungry. I will be in directly, thank you Mother, Father, Aryn."

Aryn looked surprised, not knowing that Anatoly realized she was there. They turned and went in the house. Anatoly sat there still as could be. Mother and Father assured Aryn, "He's fine, Aryn. You did a good job. He's just got a lot on his mind."

Father put his hand around Aryn's shoulder. "Come on Aryn, we will get his favorite food." They all went in the kitchen and laid out the food they had brought home with them.

Anatoly, sitting there motionless began to whistle, and the birds returned. They came near, not afraid. Aryn looked back and noticed, wondering. As they sat down to eat, Anatoly opened the door and walked in like nothing ever happened.

Mother said, "There's my happy little boy, come and sit. Are you thirsty?" Anatoly quickly ate his food, drank his drink and asked to be excused to his room to email PaPa.

"PaPa, I learned so much today. Communication is much more than words. Its pitches and motions, or no motions, but tone. It's all relevant to language, especially in the animals that are simple. They learn only their own language but people learn other languages, and we can learn animals' language. It is easier. They don't have so many things to say. I don't think they learn history or math or to write but every generation learns the same language. If it's a bird…sounds, whistles, motions. They're not afraid if you don't make motions, they don't know….. This page of my journal may be the key to us learning this language; that it's backwards.

Your one and only grandson,

Anatoly Vladimir Voss

P.S. See you soon."

Anatoly looked over some languages that he had been working on. Writing some, reciting some, he lay on the bed not changing his clothes, or taking off his shoes or turning the blankets down. Lying on his pillow, he thought with his eyes closed and fell off to sleep. If Anatoly got two hours of sleep in a row, his mind was rested enough to take on a new day. He awoke early in the morning hours before the sun came up. He sat quietly as he read the daily events of his grandFather at Lake Vostok.

Anatoly determined he would learn this language that PaPa wanted him learn. If nothing else, he wanted to be able to memorize it and say and form the words the way that it sounded from the tape his grandFather sent him. It took better than a year of not understanding any of the words, but committing them to memory. If this is the only way PaPa will let me go to Russia, he determined, I will do this.

On a summer day, Aryn came to Anatoly's door knocking. She cracked the door, "Anatoly can I come in?"

"Entre' Aryn Paige." On his computer, Anatoly's back was toward the door.

"Anatoly, come and eat your breakfast. Mother and Father have left for work. What do you say that we go on an adventure?"

Anatoly stared into his computer, working diligently. He stopped, held up his right index finger and said, "I AM on an adventure. If you will help me, we could get there sooner."

Finally, Aryn stated, "What is it? I'm all ears, Anatoly. Let's go. Where are we going? What are we doing? Anatoly talk to me. You've been busy this whole time. It seems like forever. What are we going to do? What's next on the mission?"

Anatoly stopped and turned around, looking solemnly at Aryn. "We are going to Russia."

"Russia?" Aryn said, repeating the word time and again. "Do your Mother and Father know of this?"

"Oh yes," Anatoly exclaimed. They will be going too. PaPa needs us!"

"PaPa… you're going to see PaPa in Russia?" Aryn was excited. "My sister will be there too?"

Almost ignoring Aryn's excitement, Anatoly calmly stated, "We have a job to do. PaPa, the Admiral, is counting on us." Anatoly took the day to tell Aryn what he knew, what he gathered, but of the real mission, he did not know.

So Aryn began to help Anatoly compile his papers, work on his language, and seriously began to learn. That renewed Anatoly's excitement. She believed him! She helped him with research.

"The Admiral and Captain Stacy, your sister, are finished with the expedition for this year at Lake Vostok and they are going to

Russia. When we get there, PaPa is going to show me his journal of the expedition into the Lake. He's going to let me see his journal. He promised! He is supposed to call Mother and Father so they can make arrangements."

That evening when Mother and Father got home, they brought Anatoly into the living room and called for Aryn. They sat them on the couch to talk things over. Father was pacing the floor.

"Anatoly," Father started, "Anatoly, I spoke to your grandFather today. It seems that your correspondence with him has lead him to believe that you would be an essential part of his mission in Russia and he wants us all to be there. Before I could speak to my boss about the matter, my boss came to me with transfer papers and severance pay. It seems that I have a job in Russia as well. And, Aryn, I don't know what your part in this is, but it seems we are all going to Russia."

Aryn could barely contain herself. She was so excited. She let out a squeal. "An adventure for all of us," Aryn said. "Shall I go pack?"

"Just a minute," Mr. Voss said sternly. Looking at her kindly, he asked, "Do you know what this is about, Aryn?"

Sheepishly Aryn answered, "Well I only know what Anatoly has told me over the past few months."

Father looked to Anatoly, "So this was all yours and your grandFather's doings?"

Anatoly didn't respond, he just sat there as if he was completely innocent.

Mother stood up, "We would like to know what this is about. We can't just pack up our lives, leave everything behind, and go on an adventure like we are children."

Father reached over and put his hand on her shoulder, "Now, Mother let's not be hasty. We sort of knew this day would come." Finally, Anatoly, blurted out, "PaPa won't tell me until I get there. He's afraid that....I don't know, he can't tell me. He kept saying, when I'm older, when you are ready."

"Well, son, are you ready? Father said.

"I think so," Anatoly said in Russian.

Just then Father and Anatoly began to banter back and forth in Russian, excluding Mother and Aryn. Mother reached up and squeezed Father's arm. "Father, you know I don't like it when you two do this."

Father looked back at Mother and said, "I'm sorry dear, let's sleep on this tonight. We will have a clearer head tomorrow. This is a lot to happen in one night."

Aryn again squealed and ran to her room to pack. Anatoly didn't care to pack anything but went back to his computer and began to email PaPa.

Meanwhile, the Admiral and Captain Davis flew solo to Russia. The teams would follow them a day or two behind from Lake Vostok, the expedition being finished and recorded. Arriving in Russia, they were met by countless officers and scientists, their quarters being made ready on the base.

There was a lot to prepare to gain clearance for his son and daughter- in -law, Mara Stacy's sister, and especially Anatoly. There was a lot of convincing to be done. But with help of Anatoly's daily emails, others began to be convinced, as the Admiral was, that Anatoly might make a difference in their mission, the Russian mission.

No one was able to communicate with their captive as of yet. Their captive seemed to be growing weak and they didn't know what else to do. The daily communication between the captive Leviathan and man, was that of the same story day-in-day-out, first in Russian, then this language. The Admiral had taken the Leviathan language and recorded it backwards to no avail. The Admiral's journal was published throughout the base for many of the authorized officers and scientists that had access to reading this classified material. Anatoly would read it when he arrived.

Arrangements were made. Captain Stacy Davis was just as excited as the Admiral. She would be with her sister again. She missed her sister as much as the Admiral missed Anatoly. It was difficult for the Admiral to obtain security clearance for all four, but he did get it. He sent the tickets for them to come to Russia. He sent his security team to get the young lad, his parents, and his sitter to bring them directly to the Russian base. They were greeted by a great team who were all anxious to meet Anatoly, this prodigy child they had heard so much about.

When they arrived, you would have thought Anatoly was a king or other dignitary. As they disembarked, Aryn looked about and stated, "Who are all these people? Who are they coming to see?"

As they got closer to the crowd, they all were waiting for Anatoly's first response. He spoke in Russian loudly to the crowd, "I am happy to make your acquaintance and to be at your service." Many chuckled at this coming from a five year old. They were taken to a briefing room where the Admiral would be able to tell them all about this mission, not knowing how they would respond to their only child being taken into a room and exposed to the language of this captive they had held for these years.

They saw the video and Anatoly recited the video in both the Russian language and the Leviathan language. Some of the scientists who had been around, watched Anatoly form these words…something they could not do…something they could not learn.

Aryn Paige and Mother Voss were astounded and afraid. Father wondered "What is this image?" There was too much to take in all at once for the first time hearing of it. But Anatoly knew ALL of it and wasn't afraid a bit. With his child-like faith, he understood and felt compassion for this captive and wished to immediately see the Leviathan.

The Admiral keeping charge of the crowd, stated, "We must talk of these things this evening. It may be tomorrow that Anatoly meets the Leviathan."

Aryn shrieked and was afraid for Anatoly. She blurted out without thinking, "I will go with him!" But she didn't really want to. She just didn't want Anatoly to be alone.

Anatoly turned and looked straight into her eyes which he rarely did, "Aryn Paige Davis, it's alright, I'm not afraid."

Mother Voss sat as if in shock. Father was dumbfounded as well.

Not able to form sentences or even form the words…it was beyond their comprehension.

The next day the security team came for Anatoly. The Admiral assured his son and daughter-in-law, "I will be with him. It will be okay."

Aryn turned and looked at the Admiral and said, "He's not afraid, that will help won't it? "Will it PaPa Vladimir?"

"That's right."

They arrived just in time for the Leviathan to tell his spell-binding story. They took Anatoly in the great room and sat him in a chair just out of reach of flame or limb. The Admiral stepped back into the corner, into the shadows and waited. The Leviathan thumped his tail to the floor to symbolize escape. He would have thumped it to the ceiling, but his tail was chained as well. His neck and feet all fastened to the floor with great chains, limiting movement. Just enough comfort as to not get momentum. He could not pull at his chains or their foundation. Then settling down, looking straight into Anatoly's eyes, the Leviathan began with the story, the ancient story in Russian. Much to the surprise of the Leviathan, Anatoly began the story at the same time, his voice being more thunderous than Leviathan because of the microphones they had on him. Leviathan continued. Anatoly continued. Then something happened that they hadn't seen before. It was as if a great peace came over the Leviathan. Others had recited the story in Russian. But when it came time to recite the story in the Leviathan language, no one even dared to attempt it. Anatoly went on with it in Leviathan and a great peace came over the Leviathan, almost as if he felt he was at home. When the story was ended, the Leviathan made reference to different parts of the story in his own language. Somehow Anatoly understood. He needed help, better to say, she needed help. She was Queen or to be Queen. Queen Leviathan. There was only one way Anatoly could help her. Without anyone else knowing, he helped her plan her escape. Then Anatoly stood, picked up the chair, crashed it to the floor several times, and smiled. Looking into the Leviathan's eyes, he nodded and winked, turned and left the room.

The next room was filled with people—all astonished at what happened. All began to ask questions of Anatoly at once. He turned and grabbed onto PaPa's leg. PaPa commanded in a loud voice, "You're scaring the boy." They all hushed and stepped aside. They let PaPa and the boy through the crowd. The Admiral said, "Let me take the boy to his parents where he is more comfortable and find out what happened. Don't worry, the Captain recorded the meeting for all to see tomorrow."

The team knew the Admiral fairly well. The team had arrived and was able to see the Leviathan first hand through the observation glass. No one dared to go in the room with it. It was a horrific sight when the Leviathan cooked and ate its fish.

They had a nice dinner and everything was calm with Anatoly. Aryn was with her sister again. They were inseparable since Aryn's arrival. They all sat down to a great feast.

The Admiral said to his son and daughter-in-law, "I would like to talk to all of you after dinner." They were served the finest food. Anatoly pushed his plate away. They ignored him to see what he would do. Anatoly did not move toward his plate or ask to be excused.

The Admiral said, "What is it Anatoly?"

Anatoly looked at the Admiral and said, "It's the Leviathan."

"Oh?" the Admiral exclaimed.

Mother was about to talk and Father asked her not to. They intently and quietly listened. "What about Leviathan, Anatoly? Tell PaPa."

"She's dying."

"Dying?" everyone exclaimed.

You are not giving her enough water. She can live underwater but she cannot live out of the water this long. She needs water. Her body chemistry separates the oxygen and hydrogen and other chemicals in the water and uses it in different ways."

"Anatoly, how can you know all this, you spoke but a few words."

"Also, PaPa, her flame is getting weak.

"Her?" PaPa exclaimed.

"Yes, she's the Queen; well, she will be. But we have to let her go before they come for her. They don't mean any harm but they will come for her."

"That's impossible. We can't let her go."

"Then give her what she needs. Give her water and also she needs sulfur."

"Sulfur?" Aryn chimed in with her sister Stacy at the same time, "Sulfur?" Aryn asked, "Do you even know what sulfur is?"

"Dessert" and they all laughed. Anatoly said, "She needs it to cook her food, PaPa. You have to get her some, a lot, and water for her to swim in."

Anatoly looked at PaPa. "I will work on that tomorrow, but you must eat your food."

"Not until you promise, PaPa."

"I promise, Anatoly, I will do my best."

The next day the Admiral left early with Captain Davis. Aryn was tagging along behind. "Stacy don't leave me," she said.

"We are not leaving, Aryn, I'll see you later….soon."

Anatoly was to be brought back before the Leviathan on the next day at the same time. He went in as he did before, standing before the Leviathan. There were puddles in the room where they had sprayed the creature with water hoses. There was a pile of sulfur right next to a pile of fish. The Leviathan laid her head to the floor and looked straight toward Anatoly as he pulled his chair up and started to approach Leviathan.

PaPa shouted, "No Anatoly."

Anatoly looked at PaPa and said, "It's okay, PaPa."

The Admiral said, "Not yet, grandson."

So Anatoly turned, lifted the chair by the back and slammed it to the floor almost at the same time the Leviathan slammed her tail to the floor. Each repeated and followed each other, chair, tail, chair, tail, and finally Anatoly with the chair, sat in it backward and recited the story in Russian and in the Leviathan language.

The Leviathan was different. She got what she needed and

Anatoly told her, "They are bringing you a tank to swim in." He made motions like he had a tail, like he was in the water. The Leviathan was pleased but didn't show it. Anatoly could tell.

As Anatoly entered the next room, everyone stood. The teams that came from Russia were in the front. They all greeted Anatoly with a nod or a gesture or a soft "hello." Then one asked as PaPa came and stood beside Anatoly, "Is there anything new, Anatoly?" Anatoly grabbed a onto PaPa's pant leg, rolled it up in his fingers, held on tight, and pulled PaPa's leg toward the door.

Anatoly looked at the door, "The same thing every day." Some knew what he meant; the water and the sulfur. Everyone close enough to observe the Leviathan noticed she had renewed strength and seemed to be growing, standing more erect. Her flame was getting stronger, more blue. She couldn't wait for Anatoly to come back. Anatoly came back every day to recite the story.

One evening, PaPa was talking to Mother and Father Voss in the other room. Anatoly came in and hugged PaPa's neck and said, "Thanks PaPa, this is the best mission ever." He turned and went to his room where he kept his journal.

That evening the Admiral got a phone call. Everyone in the house could hear, his voice echoing through the chambers, "What? When? How? I see. I will be there directly. Yes, thank you." He hung up the phone.

He headed towards Anatoly's room. Before he even reached the door, he cried out, "Anatoly!" Anatoly met him at the bedroom door; everyone was out of bed by this time. "Come to the living room and sit down, Anatoly." They all sat on the couch, Anatoly sitting in Father's lap. He fidgeted with his hands.

The Admiral cleared his throat, put his hands behind his back and paced the floor a little. "Anatoly, it seems the Leviathan has escaped." Everyone except Anatoly repeated, "Escaped?" Anatoly stood, looked down, fidgeted with his fingers and didn't say a word. The Admiral got a little closer. "Anatoly, look at me." Anatoly looked up then back down. "Anatoly, continue looking at me." He looked up then down. He looked up and tried to keep looking at him, but when the Admiral began to speak, he looked down again. "Do you know anything of this?"

"No, PaPa."

Father looked up at his Father and said, "Now Anatoly has done everything you've asked him to do. He is just a boy, what could he have done?"

The Admiral looked back down at Anatoly and stated, "I'm waiting, Anatoly. It seems that she used the water somehow and the sulfur to burn the chains from her limbs and with her tail crashed holes in every wall throughout the building and escaped through them."

Anatoly, looking down at his hands, said, "Well, she needed to live PaPa."

"Anatoly, she was living just fine."

"But PaPa you can't say she was living, she was chained all over, she was drying out, she was…." his voice trailed off.

Everyone was looking at Anatoly. "So you did know something of this," Father looked down at his son. Anatoly looked at Aryn and about the room, first at Aryn, then to Stacy, then to Mother, then to Father, and back to the Admiral.

"Can I go to bed now, I'm tired."

Father, with all the patience he had, said, "Go to bed son, we will discuss this further in the morning."

The Admiral and Captain Davis got dressed and went to the base. They inquired of the people who had been monitoring, "What do the videos show, which way was it heading?"

"North, North to the Barents Sea. It seems that Leviathan can fly." "Fly?" "They followed it to the Sea."

The Admiral corrected him, "Followed her to the Sea."

They looked inquisitively at the Admiral, "Her?"

The Admiral was sorry he interrupted. "Continue, people."

"We followed her across the land, then as it; as she entered the Sea, it disappeared into the depths. We have a submarine in route, but we have no way of tracking. Admiral, what do we do?"

"Send out a search party right away. Patrol the coast in case she returns. But I don't believe she will. She knew what direction to go. She's returning to her kind."

Anatoly awoke early in the morning and opened the packages the Admiral had given him. He found a tape and thumb drives of the daily events at Lake Vostok. Anatoly sneaked off to Aryn's room, crept in by her bed and lay in the floor. He crawled his fingers up the covers and he abruptly grabbed her arm and growled "Leviathan." Aryn threw her hand over her own mouth and began to shriek, but woke and realized it was just Anatoly.

Anatoly said, "Come see what PaPa gave me." They sneaked off to his room to view what they could. "PaPa was going to tell me the story like he usally does. He's going to tell us a story about when your sister, when Mara Stacy was at Lake Vostok. Come look at the pictures of Leviathan. PaPa is standing with Leviathan, a big one, a giant one, a really big giant one."

Aryn surprisingly said, "Shut up." She looked and saw the pictures for herself.

The Admiral logged every event each day and when he returned that evening, there wasn't much of a mission in Russia any longer. They might never learn the Leviathan language.

Quiet as he came in, Aryn and Anatoly met him at the door. "PaPa, PaPa, read the story, tell the story, tell the story. We know what happened all the way to the part where you broke through the ice. Tell us the rest of the story. What happened?"

It was the first time the Admiral had laughed in days. There was nothing he could do about what had happened. He took the two kids under his arms, one under each arm and said, "After dinner, we will talk about this. Oh, this was exciting, this was an exciting day. Everyone has you to thank for this."

"You are not mad any longer?"

"I wasn't mad; I was a little disappointed that things didn't go as we planned. Maybe we will find her and now we have a better understanding of them. After dinner we will start all the stories. We can't do it all in one day. It was a grand mission, Lake Vostok."

After dinner, Aryn was on one side, Anatoly on the other side of the dinner table where PaPa sat drinking his coffee; they patiently waited. Mara Stacy looked at the children with Mother and Father Voss, and she said, "What are you two up to?" They looked up at PaPa quietly.

Stacy said, "Aryn."

Aryn looked at Stacy, she said, "The Admiral is going to tell us the story of Lake Vostok."

Stacy interrupted her and said, "Admiral."

The Admiral looked down at his plate and put his fork, spoon and his napkin on his plate. He said, "Well, the cat's out of the bag; they might as well know the rest of the story."

At this time, Mother and Father Voss were very interested as well. They all went off to Anatoly's room where they could put the pictures on the TV. Aryn turned to her sister. She was helping the maid clear some plates from the table, "Are you coming Mara Stacy?" Mara looked at her sister and smiled.

"No, Aryn, I was there, remember?"

"Oh yes, you typed it, didn't you Mara Stacy?"

Stacy said, "and gathered the recordings." Aryn turned and ran into the room so she wouldn't miss any of it.

The Admiral said, "Where should we begin; where should we begin?"

Anatoly said, "When you broke through the ice, we want to know what happened."

"Ah, yes." They all intently listened to the Admiral. He had set up the computer like a slide show of the video footage taken under the waters, through the caverns, on the land, under the lake, two miles under the ice of Lake Vostok. "The Robotics made this footage," the Admiral began. "As you can see, camera number one was suspended from the dome ceiling and tried to focus in on the shore and on the events that unfolded there. But let me point out first, camera number two that was suspended just under the waters. It was about dinner time. Some Leviathan had escaped through the hole where the water geysered out. But these Leviathan (just then on the video some Leviathan came as if they were performing for the underwater camera), they went in a small circle, then up through the depths and hit the dome ceiling with their tails right next to the hole. Then, one by one they swam to the shore as if they were playing follow the leader. Here you can see from the camera in the depths, how deep they go through the caves, breathing fire from their nostrils, lighting their paths and herding the fish. You can see how they work together. These few that were left, some smaller, a few older, had stayed behind. We supposed they went to the other lakes or somewhere deep in the caverns, but they all came to this lake at dinner time and slammed their tails to the ceiling, cracking the edges of the ice, great chunks of ice falling to the water. We had to reset the land camera so we didn't know until the last day what had happened on the land, and that was our greatest discovery! Another camera was suspended from the dome ceiling and the other one seemed to be smashed and broken. It was dark and the light wasn't sufficient. We prepared more lights and the next evening about dinner time, we had the most amazing discovery."

"The Leviathan all swam to the rocky shore one by one and laid on the shore and they all recited the same story that the young Leviathan at the lab recited. Then, look at the screen, right here, (pointing at the tv screen)now behind, emerging from behind Leviathan way up from the shores, two men came walking out of the buildings. Later we discovered they were the two Russian scientists who were lost in an expedition, sustained, and kept alive by the Leviathan. They came out to listen to the stories and communicated somewhat with Leviathan. After a few days, the expedition team was lowered into rafts, paddled ashore to meet the Russians in the caverns, mining and sustaining themselves with the daily routine of preparing food. They told us of their years there with Leviathan and how that it seemed to be an ancient city ,and how they assumed the roles of the people of the city with what was left. They had fires blowing for a blacksmith, waters pumping, mixing the salt water and fresh water into great hatcheries where they hatched the fish into great pools and grew them and fed them with scraps of fish that they had dried on the shores. "

"The Russians were very glad to see the cameras and knew that it was I who had returned to drill through. And when we lowered the men into the boats and went to the shores, the Russians met them and pulled them into the buildings, and said, 'Don't get in the way of Leviathan. They won't hurt you, they are not here to harm you, but you can't communicate with them either and you can't stop them from their daily routine.'

I went on this first expedition and asked for volunteers to go with me. No one would go, and I wouldn't let Captain Davis, Mara Stacy, go but had her manning the posts and directing the monitoring of the videos. As we communicated with these Russians, we had all day before the Leviathan would return. They took us deep into the buildings that went into the sides of the cliffs, fresh water coming down from the cliffs. They had much to tell us, much to show us. With their blacksmith tools and materials, they were making covers for the claws and for the teeth of Leviathan, made out of precious metals. Somehow they figured out from drawings on the walls, which metals to mix. All the Leviathan that escaped had their teeth and their claws capped with iron and gold, ready for battle. I asked the two Russians how they were forced to do this, and they merely stated that they weren't forced to do it. They did it in trade. The Leviathan provided for them, and they provided for Leviathan the things they needed. Then they took us into the caverns and showed us what they had been mining… jewels and gold ,and all sorts of precious minerals."

Aryn blurted out, "A treasure, really a treasure?"

Anatoly looked at Aryn and had his hand over his mouth so he wouldn't interrupt and widened his eyes toward Aryn and put his hand on his mouth and mumbled, "Mmmm. Mmm." Aryn put her hand over her mouth and listened intently, hoping she didn't make the Admiral to lose his place.

"Dinner time came and the Russians knew it was close…they could feel what time it was. They led us back to the buildings on the shore, and we were watching through the open window as the Leviathan returned. They do this every evening, the Russians said. They sort of understood that they have been captive here for thousands of years and it's what they were commanded to do. The largest of the Leviathan that remain go first. Just then, exploding from the water, a great Leviathan thrust himself straight to the ceiling and turned abruptly, cracking his tail to the ceiling. The thunder echoed through the caverns and startled everyone as it rumbled through our hearts and our bodies. Just then, another, and another, hitting their mark. You could see the dome ceiling riddled with steel claws, where the Leviathan left them in the ceiling. The Russians told me, they thought it was practice. Practice for what? I asked. Practice for battle. They all swam in a line to the shore, one by one and plumped their enormous bodies on the hard sharp shards and rocks of the shore. They knew…they could smell that other people were there. The behemoth Leviathan that first arrived breathed flames of fire that leaped from his nostrils and mouth in a straight line toward the wall nearest him. The Russians said, 'I think they know you are here. I think we should show ourselves.' They all filed through the door and stood in line and at the same time the Russians started the story just as Anatoly had done. "

"One of the smaller Leviathan walked over to us and flared his nostrils right in my face. I was trembling and some of the other scientists turned and ran back into the caverns. The two Russians laughed. They said, 'They mean you no harm.' But it was very uncomfortable and it was hard not to fear these greatest of creatures. They turned and lay on the shores and started their stories. The Russians walked toward them and watched."

"The Russians persuaded us to stay there for the evening, not to ascend back through the ice. They took us back into the rooms, and they had quite comfortable quarters. They had fashioned together what they could. There was some plant life that grew in the side of the hill through the rocks by the fresh water streaming down; plants that had never been seen before. It was a spectacular event. We took samples of everything we could. "

"The next morning as the Leviathan plunged into the waters, we took our raft back, communicated with the surface, and all of us escaped through the hole. The two Russians went first. We ascended and descended a few more times and took these photographs, he pointed. We tried to communicate with the Leviathan that were there. The two Russians wished to return to the Leviathan, but I refused them. We brought them back to Russia. Would you like to meet them, Anatoly?"

Anatoly removed his hand from his mouth. He said, "Me? Boy, would I! I want to go there." They all laughed.

Mother said, "Now son, it is much too dangerous."

PaPa said, "There is much more to tell and to show you. We will save it for another night. Get some rest, Anatoly and Aryn. Is there anyone else who would like to go meet the Russians tomorrow?"

Mother said, "I don't speak Russian, I do not wish to go."

The Admiral said, "As you wish."

Aryn looked at the Admiral and said, "Me? I can go? Me? I don't speak Russian, either."

"Nevertheless, if you wish to go you may, the Admiral said. "We can show you where the Leviathan broke out."

"Another adventure, I would love to go." Aryn jumped up and grabbed PaPa's arm. "I would love to go."

"Fine! Get some rest," said the Admiral.

CHAPTER 12

The Visit with the Russians

THE NEXT MORNING, ANATOLY WAS up early working on his journal. It was still dark outside and he heard some movement in the kitchen. "I bet that is PaPa," he thought out loud. As he quietly slunk into the kitchen, he surprised PaPa and grabbing his leg, he let out a growl.". .Leviathan"...! ! PaPa pretended to be frightened even though he heard Anatoly coming.

Whispering as to not wake anyone, Anatoly began to ask, "PaPa when will we go speak to the two Russians"?

PaPa said, "Dinner time would be a good time, since that is when the three of them are used to meeting with the Leviathan and reciting their story."

Anatoly looked puzzled, and then asked, "Three of them?"

"Yes Anatoly, remember the lady scientist that the Leviathan rescued? She and the two men came every evening to the Leviathan and recited with him."

"Her, PaPa, her."

"Ah yes Anatoly her."

"But PaPa I did not see them when I was with the Leviathan, where were they?"

"They were behind the glass, son. Some days the room was lit so Leviathan could see them, and speakers installed so he...or I mean she could hear them. It seemed to make her feel more at home. Now I must go prepare for you to come to the base; your Father will bring you and Aryn later."

"Ok, PaPa; I will see you there."

The day seemed to go by quickly. A lot of preparations go into such a big event. And Father must convince Mother, Anatoly was not in trouble for what he did. They sat on the couch, Father stroking Mother's raven black hair, "Now MaMa" he started softly, we're not even sure that the Leviathan's escape was a direct result of what Anatoly told them to do. And besides, it is best for the creature that it is returned to its own kind."

Mother gasped as she imagined further, "What if they come looking for him, the Leviathan might have something more they need of Anatoly."

"Now, MaMa, the Leviathan seemed to like Anatoly, but I figure it will end up Anatoly making an adventure of looking for Leviathan."

Mother gasped again when she heard this and began to cry. Father tried to console her, but no matter what he said it seemed to upset her more. "MaMa, I mean when he is much older." Mother buried her face into her hands and ran off to her room crying.

Anatoly came into the room just as Mother ran out ,and he asked of his Father, "Am I in trouble DaDa?"

"No Anatoly, Mother just needs some time alone. Yes that is it; it is time to go anyway. Go fetch Aryn from her room. We don't want to be late."

As they walked out front there was a car waiting to take them to the base. Father looked down at Anatoly (still holding Aryn's hand, from dragging her through the house) pointing at the car he said, "Your grandFather thinks of everything does he not?"

On the way, in the car, they barely spoke a word. Anatoly just peered out the window and noticed how the sky was so different than any place he had been.

PaPa met them at the gate and got in the car with them, without missing a beat. Aryn asked PaPa, how to say hello in Russian and other things she wished to say. PaPa chuckled, and put his hand on Aryn's shoulder and said, "Just stay by me I will let you know what is going on."

Aryn let out a big sigh in anticipation of the day. Then looking up into the Admiral's face said, "That would be good, PaPa."

As they arrived at the military facility, it was noised throughout the base of the Admiral's arrival. Everyone was snapping to attention saluting the Admiral's vehicle and passing him through to the facility where the Leviathan had been kept. The two Russians lived there and did not wish to leave that facility as long as the Leviathan was kept there.

Everyone wished to see the prodigy (Anatoly) and it looked as if they lined the halls, just to see him. Anatoly walked behind PaPa holding Aryn's hand (he said so she would not get lost). As Anatoly passed people, he handed out (mostly in Russian) retorts and greetings as they came to his keen mind; he decided to whom was deserving of a comment or a greeting, "good morning, pleasant day, I remember you, how about that Leviathan, nice salute, good morning, beautiful skies here in Russia."

As they passed through the corridors, there became less and less people as the halls passed to more secure areas. Finally they reached the room. The two Russian men were already there, waiting anxiously. They met in the room with the big glass wall overlooking the room where the Leviathan had been.

Anatoly was behind the Admiral as they entered the room staying hid from view. The two men chuckled, "Do not be afraid!"

Anatoly stepped out in front, and said in Russian, "I am not afraid, good morning."

Aryn recognized the words and also blurted out a kind of rough "good morning," in Russian, and could not remember any of the other words she had practiced and wished to say. She looked up at the Admiral for support, and he gave her a comforting smile and a nod.

Anatoly walked straight up to the two Russians, shook each of their hands and said, "I am very pleased to meet you both." He immediately started to converse with them both, as if they were old friends. "I was anxious to meet the two bravest men in the world that lived with the Leviathan."

Just then at that same time, someone started a recording, and as if like clockwork, the two Russians turned toward the empty room looking through the glass, and along with the recording recited the Leviathan story, history, and the prophesy. Anatoly chimed in with them. Aryn looked at PaPa puzzled, and then pulled two chairs away from the table the Russians and Anatoly were sitting at. Anatoly stood up in the chair that was with its back to the table looking down into the room, remembering when the Leviathan was there.

Aryn stood by PaPa as he sat down in the chair he had pulled away from the table. Aryn leaned to PaPa's ear and whispered, "Why are they still doing that? The Leviathan is gone!"

PaPa whispered back, "It has become habit, and maybe a form of comfort." As they had began, the door behind them quietly and gently swung open. A fit and small woman entered the room, walked up to the glass and recited with the three that had already begun. Anatoly knew who it was and smiled at her. As they finished, Anatoly jumped down from his chair, went to the window, grabbed the lady's hand and said, "I know who you are, you are famous...to me." They all laughed. Anatoly had many questions, and the Russians diligently answered. Then without hesitation both Russians announced to Anatoly that they were going back to the Antarctic to live with the Leviathan, and they wished to convince others to go as well.

But no one had seen what they saw, and convincing anyone was difficult, or nearly impossible to say the least. Anatoly said, "I wish to go too." And he glanced around at PaPa as did the others in the room. PaPa put his head down, and frowned. Anatoly then said, "When I get older then I will come, I will take over for the Admiral and have my own drilling."

The Admiral stood to his feet and in a commanding voice said, "It is much too dangerous for any one. Much too dangerous. We have still yet to analyze all the samples we have brought back, to know if it is safe."

The men were almost offended at this and stood and said, "We are healthy, and you...left us there for almost two years. In fact, we are through being observed, and we will be leaving the facility soon, and when we get the finances we will return to the city under the ice."

Anatoly turned to the Russian lady that was rescued, to see what her view was. She began to quietly speak, "Leviathan means no harm. They helped me—they... she saved my life. Anatoly, are you certain our Leviathan was, is a female?"

Anatoly stood erect, stuck his chest out and stated "I am certain. And not just a female, but the Queen, and she must return too, so she will never be killed. And we will help her to return."

The Admiral walked over to Anatoly and quietly said, "Anatoly that is quite enough."

Anatoly looked up at PaPa and calmly said, "But PaPa, I know where to find them, it is in their story, and we can find them!" Then he looked back at the two Russians still standing at the table, and repeated, "We will, we will find them."

The two Russians sheepishly looked at one another; the older slightly shook his head, and turning to the Admiral said, "Admiral we would like very much to speak to your grandson again, if it is convenient, sir."

The Admiral took a slow pause to regain his usual temperance. "Gentlemen (he spoke in a low calming voice), it appears you have inspired my grandson to a great undertaking that will take much thought and preparation. I will be in contact with you tomorrow. Captain Davis will be here in the AM to make arrangements for better surroundings, for such a meeting."

The Russian lady had been quiet, still peering through the glass. Anatoly looked up grabbing her by the hand and asked,"Russian lady can I see you again too?"

With a kind of half smile, softly she said,"Ola,...my name is Ola, and I would be pleased to see you again, Anatoly." Without saying another word to anyone else, she slipped out the door, giving a slight nod toward Aryn. Aryn had been sitting so quietly she did not think anyone had noticed her. After Ola nodded toward her, she turned and said in Russian, "Pleased to meet you ." The whole time she was sitting there, she had practiced it; since everyone was speaking in Russian, and she didn't understand a word of it any way.

At this, Anatoly stood at attention, saluted the two Russian men said, "Good evening." He did an about face, and marched toward the door. Then grabbing Aryn by the hand as he passed by her,he dragged her into the hall. Then he commanded in English, "Left turn...MARCH-hup-two-three-four." And they marched all the way to the automobile, saluting some as he passed. Aryn dragged behind trying to keep in step, snickering with her hand on her mouth.

CHAPTER 13

Leviathan Unites

LEVIATHAN EVER CONTINUED NORTHWARD...SINCE THE escape. Lead Leviathan ever pressing forward, not looking back to see if any was following, but leaving a clearly marked path. He traveled on the bottoms of the seas and oceans, moving reefs and ground as he pulled himself along. Leviathan that followed also pulled themselves along in the same manner the same places, even the same footholds, trying to keep up with Lead. Traveling for days on end, they did not need to come up for air. Looking about, the young Leviathan (that were born in captivity) saw many new sights, having to break free from the mindset of the mundane daily chores, and stories, and to and fro travels (though the domain was vast) and had many new thoughts. It was an experience that was completely new, never to be new again. Even Lead and the larger Ancients were reminded of times past, the ocean floors recognizable and familiar.

But every evening and at the same time, they recited the story in their minds. Lead would strike his tail spikes hard against whatever object or ground he was near and all Leviathan would reciprocate. Encouraging themselves with the story, everything coming to fruition. If any Leviathan was near another, they would glance stones or coral or sand from their scales, struck up by the one in front (a sort of game they ever played at home).

It was then that the Leviathan born in captivity understood the stories and training and ever encouraged themselves to persevere for days without cause; it was all for these days and nights of travel. The Leviathan's true power revealed, to themselves as well; they became great over and over. They chanted in their minds, thinking of the greatness of their race. By reason of breaking, they purify themselves. He maketh the deep to boil like a pot: he maketh the sea like a pot of ointment. He maketh a path to shine after him; (one) would think the deep (to be) hoary. Upon Earth there is not his like, who is made without fear.

The routine events were much like at home, except the traveling never stopped. And the new events were fleeting. The hunting in a pack was also fleeting but invigorating. The fish at home was good practice (though the fish schooled like a herd trained). The hunt of each prey differed. The seals had a mind of their own, and the tactics to capture them were the same end result, cornering, pushing them right to one another's clutches.

Then they came upon an American nuclear submarine. But instead of investigating, they were led away from it. Following Lead they turned abruptly away, correcting their course miles later. They avoided the Sonar with a zig zag pattern, completely avoiding being detected again. The Sonar from the submarine was going crazy with what looked like to be underwater ships passing. An improbability at the speed they were traveling. Nevertheless they were marked as ships. They alerted the whole American Navy of their Northern trajectory.

Leviathan could feel the Sonar deflecting from their scales and flesh and did not understand it fully. But Lead remembered a day that was a major event that he intended to add to their daily story, but never dared to (since it was his order) as long as they were in captivity, to not communicate with words, other than the daily story, history, and events. So to better formulate a plan, Lead decided to make a short detour and add this major event to the story and to give each Leviathan a better understanding of communication by words.

When they got a great distance from the submarine, Lead turned toward a small island, and the waters were becoming shallow, the coral reefs ejecting from the ocean floor out of the water. Each leviathan wondered the change in plan, but willingly followed. All Leviathan saw Lead communicating with second Leviathan and were astonished, knowing it was forbidden; that was made clear that it was forbidden.

It was early evening and the natives of the island were fishing the shores with their nets. Some were lighting torches along the beach and taking fish from the nets and putting them in baskets. Some natives standing on the shore saw out past the coral reef, where the waters lit up like with fire, and appeared to be boiling. The natives were gaining the attention of all that were with them, pointing at the sight, when suddenly, in a moment's time, a great beast rose from the sea abruptly, startling them, then another beast and another. The fishermen fell backward and fainted at the sight. Some were still in the water, when the Leviathan saw them fainting, they rushed in a line, pushing a great wave in front of them. This pushed all the natives with the nets and all that they had up onto the shore. This caused the faint to awake, and floundering around, they managed to get to their feet and ran for the village, forsaking the nets.

Still in a line, the Leviathan pushed with their front legs and chest, a great mound of sand, in front of them all the way to the tree line, covering to the top of some of the shorter trees. This they did to gain privacy from the natives.

None of the natives were hurt, and they all went to hide in their huts. Some dared to peer through the door to see if the beasts were coming after them, but after a while they heard no more. Some ran into the jungle in the night, preferring to face the night jungle than to see this beast again.

With the moonlit evening, it was still brighter than day at home (in the icy prison, with the luminous dome ceiling). Leviathan all gathered on the shore to chant the story. But before they could begin, Lead stumbled over words that would ever be an addition to the story to recite but only in their language. So in their native tongue he began.

This day I, Lead, was reminded of another day, like today, when we turned from mans iron under water ship. The wave of pressure we felt, and heard in our heads from the craft was the same as we felt through the waters of our home, on that day (in our home). I, Lead knew it, when we felt the pressure on our scales and it almost stunned with the force. And it tasted like metal in the mouth. Pressing the fires of our bosom and caused the flame within to burst uncontrollably. Lead knew it was mans devices and formed for the first time a question. Never before had I, Lead, thought of a day in the past. Since there was no man to ask or communicate with, I, Lead kept my question and remembered it not again until a day of communication with the two Russian men. Then I mentioned that day. I, Lead was able to convey with Russian words, motions, and gestures, my question.

With pictures in the sand and with many words (some which were not understandable), they explained to me the device they had invented to cause such pressure of invisible waves.

Lead looked up into the sky, and they all did likewise. Somehow they direct the waves to the stars around but above the Earth, and with devices they have placed up there, they direct its attention in waves to where they point. The waves travel to the place they send it and back again to tell what is there.

All Leviathan looked puzzled and one questioned, "What is a star?"

"Communication can be good, Lead responded, and now some Leviathan have questions, but that is not the event or what I wish to add to the story. The day I am remembering is the day I communicated with man of a memory. And this day I, Lead, remembered the day my question was answered by the two Russian men."

"And we are convinced, we will never understand man's devices, and we should not try, but rather Leviathan must ever avoid man at all cost, more than ever before because of the devices."

"Lead could barely remember how to formulate a plan, so the plan was made with the two Russians to help to save our Queen. The two Russians knew they would one day return home to be with the people of the North. So we devised a plan of rescue. The two Russians wish to return to the city we love and they have learned to love. And they want to recruit men and female type to help with the operations of the hatcheries and smith and mining jobs. But some men will grow greedy of our resources there, and wish to leave to get gain and return to the North to prosper there. So each one of us have a golden claw cover to bring to the two Russians to advance their expedition."

In return, the two Russians have told us details of how we may free our Queen and escape under the cover of night when men will be sleeping. Leviathan will come ashore where they will mark with six torches and leave a map or they will be there themselves to instruct us." They all understood they must go first to rescue the Queen, then they would unite with the other offspring that may or may not have survived in the North of the Barents Sea.

So the plan was hatched and was conveyed to all Leviathan. And Leviathan's thoughts and communications would never be the same. All began to gain knowledge and increase communications skills and all would begin to form questions and to think more freely (in return probably some might stray).

So the Leviathan left the little Island. All understood the plan more perfectly. And all were developing new thoughts as they traveled the ocean floor around the land masses.

The two Russian men daily traveled to the shore to plan for the arrival of the Leviathan. They had free access to come and go from the base. No one questioned them. With what they had been through (for nearly two years), it was assumed they needed the time alone. At the base they only discussed the events of their captivity. None knew of their communication and plans with the Leviathan.

Nor did any expect they were conspiring to forever change the fate of a forgotten species.

The two Russians secured a cave (a sort of lease arrangement), with the Russian government. They had buildings erected in a manner which made people think they were a monument of sorts (which was really a crude map), due North of the base and the distance clocked, to free the Queen of the Leviathan.

Torches were lit nightly on the shores of their new temporary home. No one suspected anything, they explained, this ritual they did nightly in their home under the ice in the Antarctic. The cave in the cliffs, behind the Russians' home had been excavated and enlarged to accommodate guests of behemoth proportions. Not to accommodate a stay, but to enable the Leviathan to store the golden horns from their claws (that they themselves fashioned as the role of blacksmith assumed in captivity).

They also secretly purchased a large sea-going vessel with gold and jewels they smuggled to Russia with their gear. They spent all they had and borrowed all they could, knowing they would have the gold the Leviathan were bringing to afford their expedition.

The excavating equipment they acquired would suffice to aid them in removing the gold to smelt for transport to sell. They need such equipment, for some claw horns were ten feet tall. Leviathan came to the shores the Russians told them of. There were only five torches burning. As planned, they would wait until the next evening, when there would be six torches, signifying the day and night. There would be a skeleton crew on the base. Lead came ashore and communicated with the two Russians as they lit the six torches that evening.

The two Russians left a clear path of solid sulfur rocks which was easy for the Leviathan to follow, glowing in the evening light. They stayed in a straight line following Lead. They approached the fence surrounding the base, and the fence laid down flat under their enormous weight. As they approached the walls, great sections of the walls were quickly and quietly in Lead's grasp and handed backward through the line from one set of claws to another set of claws, and laid along the path, making a kind of foothold along the way toward the shore. They covered their tracks as to astound the men that would find what was done in the morning. In a matter of seconds, they were through all the walls straight to Queen's large open room. Queen showed them the chains binding her legs and tail to the floor by breathing flames onto the restraints. Immediately Lead knew what to do, and with a quick breath, fire leaped from his nostrils and melted the restraints. The flames did not hurt the Queen as they tempered one another's scales in such a manner always at home in captivity. Then she was almost propelled into the air carried along by all the Leviathan.

Back to the water's edge, one by one the Leviathan came back to the shore. They stopped by the cave and heated the golden claws off them, sort of flicked them into the cave, and returned to the sea, without so much as a good-bye or even a glance back. They disappeared as quickly as they appeared, leaving a pile of gold in the cave, more gold than the two Russians would ever be able to use. Watching as the last Leviathan descended into the sea, they immediately began to have the gold loaded on their ship to fund the expedition back to the Antarctic. They did not know in what direction the Leviathan went or how to find them, but they just moved forward with the plan.

Leviathan traveling back to the bottom of the sea, headed straight for the ancient hiding place of the young they had left so many ages ago, not knowing what they would find or if any Leviathan survived in the North during their captivity.

CHAPTER 14

Anatoly calls for Queen Leviathan

THE NEXT EVENING, ALL THE Vosses were home having dinner together with Mara Stacy and Aryn Paige Davis. After dinner was finished, Anatoly asked his Mother if he could be excused. She nodded. So he wiped his mouth with his cloth napkin, placed it on his plate, and quietly pulled his chair back. He crept around to the end of the table and quietly he got the Admiral's attention. With his sleeve being pulled down, PaPa leaned down toward Anatoly to hear what he was softly asking.

"PaPa can we go speak to the two Russian men again? Please, PaPa, can we? What are their names? No one told me their names. I need to see them. I need to ask them some questions. Can we go PaPa?"

The Admiral put his arm around the boy's neck and whispered back, "I will arrange it grandson." Satisfied with the answer, Anatoly ran off to his room to work on his computer.

Aryn also excused herself and followed Anatoly to his room. She did not quite hear what Anatoly was talking to PaPa about. She was going to find out, she thought, as she went through the doorway.

Mara Stacy was sitting next to the Admiral and heard what Anatoly had asked of him. When she knew no one was listening, she began to speak to the Admiral. "Admiral, I have been in contact with personnel at the military installation, and everyone is a bit more than bafricated at this little troubadour that helped aid in the escape of their project."

The Admiral looked Stacy in the eyes, and leaning toward her, in a low voice, he exclaimed, "Now Captain, we don't know for certain the boy's efforts aided in any such thing."

"What are you implying Admiral?" the Captain asked with a raised eyebrow.

The Admiral replied, "I want to speak to the two Russian men myself, I believe they know more than they are letting on. I am sure they will readily agree to meet. They have expressed an interest in meeting with Anatoly; just myself and the boy alone, mind you Captain."

"Yes sir, I understand, only I have contacted the base this morning and it appears the two Russian men have permanently left the observatory. Just last evening they received their walking papers. They are living nearby on the Northern shores, retired. Nevertheless, I am sure I can find them and set up an appointment."

The Admiral sat up straight and pushed his plate away. Then stated, "I am sure I can count on you, Captain, you are always so very proficient. I would like to make it for tomorrow evening if you could arrange it. Thank you Captain Davis."

"If you will excuse me Admiral, I will make the necessary arrangements," she said as she turned to walk away. Then turning back she said, "Oh and Admiral if you don't need me tomorrow, I would like to go sightseeing with Aryn and Mrs. Voss. We will make arrangements to meet you to drop off Anatoly." With arrangements made, the Admiral left for the military installation that evening to tie up loose ends and sort out some details for next summers' trip to the Antarctic. The next morning Mrs. Voss was in the kitchen. Mr. Voss walked in dressed for work. As he was handed his coffee, Mrs. Voss asked, "Can you go with us sightseeing today?

Over a sip of coffee, he replied, "No, some of us still work for a living." "Now Father," Mother exclaimed as she approached closer, "I was just hoping you could come and act as interpreter." Father downed his cup of coffee, kissed his wife, and then he replied as he headed for the door, "You have Mara Stacy and Anatoly. You will be fine."

In the morning, Aryn came back into Anatoly's room, knowing he would be on his computer. "Anatoly are you going to get ready to go?"

Without looking up from the computer, Anatoly replied, "I am ready to go. Besides I am going with PaPa today."

Aryn sat in a chair next to him, trying to get his undivided attention, and blurted out, "PaPa left last evening, and Stacy told me your Mother wants you with her today, and we are dropping you off to PaPa later."

This got Anatoly's attention, and he turned about in his chair, and looked up into Aryn's eyes. Then he said, "Aryn I have something to ask you."

Interrupting him, Aryn said, "I also have something to ask you." Then without hesitation, she started asking away, "When we went to go talk to the two Russians the other day, what happened? It seemed as though PaPa got a little irritated, for a minute."

Anatoly jumped to his feet and leaned in toward Aryn. He lightly grabbed her by both arms and asked his question, "Will you go with me to live at Lake Vostok?"

Aryn was more than stunned. Forgetting her question, she looked down into Anatoly's serious eyes. All she could muster to say was, "Stop Anny, you are frightening me! Besides no one can live there, it is too cold in the Antarctic."

Anatoly sat back down and turning back to his computer, answered, "Not at Lake Vostok; it is the fountain of youth." Aryn sat quiet, not knowing what to say. She knew he would never let it go, once he made up his mind.

She stood and put her hand on his shoulder and tried to say something genuine. "Anatoly you will feel differently when you are older," not really believing it herself after she said it. Anatoly just sat at his computer as if they had not even had the conversation.

Aryn did not know what else to say, and stuttered, "I…I have not thought about what I want to do with my life. If…I…, Anatoly talk to me." Anatoly in a soft kind voice said, "I thought you were doing your life." A tear came to Aryn's eye as she turned to leave the room, she thought, "This boy will soon be a man, and what kind of man will he be?"

Mother called for everyone to come to breakfast. Anatoly instantly appeared from under the counter, and startled his Mother. Climbing up onto the stool, he asked, "Mother, I thought I was to go with PaPa today?"

Mother replied, "Now Anatoly, how would we get along without you today? My little linguist." Knowing the answer would not satisfy him, she added, "Your grandFather had to work, so he asked if we could meet him later so you can accompany him to the Russians' house."

This satisfied Anatoly, then he asked, "Can Aryn come with us?"

Just then Mara Stacy came around the corner, with Aryn just behind her. She answered for Mrs. Voss, "Oh no, Aryn is all mine today." She quickly took three giant steps over toward Anatoly. Reaching out she tickled Anatoly under his arms, then continued, "Mine I say, all mine. You got that little Mr. Voss, all mine today." They all laughed and sat down to eat breakfast.

When they finished, a car was waiting for them out front. Anatoly ran to his room, to retrieve his questions he had been preparing all morning for the two Russians later that day. He folded it neatly and put it in his pocket.

As they toured around town, Anatoly was between Mother and Aryn holding their hands until their palms were all sweaty. Stacy spoke to everyone they came in contact with while Anatoly translated and explained what was going on. The day was short with three of his favorite people with him all day. He almost forgot about the evening ahead, and all of the sudden Mother said, "Let's go, it is time to meet the Admiral." They got into the automobile and were under way. Anatoly put his hand on his pocket to make sure the folded paper was in his pocket. Feeling it through his pants, he started to get anxious, and bounced in his seat, waving his hands as he bounced. Mother softly said to him, "Anatoly, you should not excite yourself so, we will arrive soon enough."

As they turned the corner, the Admiral was standing by his automobile with his hands folded in front of him, waiting patiently. His usual security formed a perimeter around him and the automobile. Mother got out and approached the Admiral, pulling her sunglasses to her nose, still holding them between her fingers. She looked up into his eyes, and boldly stated, "Admiral Voss, you be extra careful with my little boy this evening."

The Admiral put his large hands firmly, but gently, on her two shoulders and with that friendly smile, assured her, in his deep assuming voice, "Always Mrs. Voss, always."

She said, "And don't give Anatoly any funny ideas about going down to that icy, no-man's land, at the bottom of the world, you call a mission."

The Admiral snapped to attention, saluted, and said, "Aye, Aye Mother, I will do my best Ma'am."

Mother smiled put her glasses back on and turned to go back to the automobile. As she passed Anatoly, she reached out and mussed up his hair, and said to him, "Be a good boy, mommy loves you," knowing he didn't like her to hug or kiss him in public.

The three ladies rode off to have dinner with Father. Anatoly got into the car with PaPa. He started bouncing up and down and waving his hands.

PaPa looked down firmly into Anatoly's eyes, and calmed him with his words, "It will be good to see the Russian scientists this evening. Are you hungry grandson?" Anatoly quickly understood that meant for him to calm himself and put his hands under his legs to hold himself calm.

The Admiral gave some instructions to the driver, and told

Anatoly, "We are going to have dinner with the two Russian men at their home this evening."

Anatoly could barely contain himself, and put his hand to his pocket, and said, "That is just perfect, PaPa, just perfect. PaPa I have some questions for them, so they are my heroes. Since I met them, they are my heroes."

Anatoly pulled his list from his pocket and carefully unfolded it.

PaPa looked down and said, "That is quite a list of questions." Anatoly quickly read the list silently, then neatly folded it again and put it back into his pocket. They rode silently for a while. Then Anatoly broke the silence with a question, "PaPa, when you go back to the Antarctic, can I go? I am older now."

The Admiral smiled and not wishing to set him off, calmly turned the blame to somewhere else, "Now son, how about when you are a teenager. I am sure your parents would not approve." Anatoly's posture fell, and he stated, "But. PaPa, I want to go now. I want Aryn to go live with me there and Mother and Father and you, PaPa. I want us all to live there and help the Leviathan, and live happily ever after."

The Admiral put his hand on Anatoly's opposite shoulder, assuring him. He said, "Now, Anatoly, you are very bright, but when you get older you will feel differently. It is all my fault for pushing you so hard to learn and to keep you active."

Anatoly blurted out, "No, I will not feel differently. I have made plans. It all makes sense; I know where I want to go. I know what I want to do."

The Admiral interrupted, "It is a very harsh environment, much too harsh for any one, much less young people." Anatoly answered, "I know, I know."

The Admiral patted him on his shoulder, "Calm down, son, we will speak to the two Russians tonight. They will affirm what I am telling you."

Anatoly said to himself, "I know, I know, I know," and looked out the window, at the sky passing by. Things got really quiet, the rest of the way there. Anatoly fell asleep, with his hand on his list.

When they arrived, Anatoly saw out the window as they approached, a relatively small house, in the midst of a vast shoreline. "Is this where they live?" Anatoly asked.

He jumped out of the car and ran toward the house, leaving PaPa behind. The Admiral got out, gave a few more orders, made some motions with his hands, and turned to join Anatoly at the door. The security team set up a perimeter, and hunkered down for a long while.

The door opened to them as the Admiral approached. One of the Russians, bending slightly, greeted them. "Ahh, Anatoly, it is nice to see you again," and held out his hand toward the little lad. As Anatoly put his tiny hand in the Russian's rather large hand, he finished with, "My name is Seth."

Anatoly shook his hand as hard as he could and said in Russian, "It is nice to meet you, Seth." The Russian stood erect, stretched his hand toward the interior, with his palm up, and said, "Come in, we have everything ready for you two, make yourselves at home." As they came out of the foyer, there was a great room. And on the back side of the room the whole wall was glass, on a curve, so you could see the whole coastline. Out the window on the shore were seven torches burning in the distance near the water's edge. There was a great table in the middle of the room. At the end, was standing the other Russian. He held out his hands toward Anatoly. "Anatoly, we are so glad you and your GrandFather could make it. I also have not told you my name. It is Victor." Anatoly approached him and shook both of his hands, "It is nice to know your name, too. Anatoly walked around him to the window. Looking out toward the water he asked, "This is where you live? Is that the Barents Sea?"

The Admiral came in with Seth by his side, Seth said, "Shall we eat?" They immediately sat, and people started coming out of both ends of the house to serve them.

Anatoly thought, "They have more people than PaPa." The Admiral spoke formally during dinner. After dinner they retired to the den to have a smoke and a drink. Anatoly had let the adults talk at dinner, but as he settled into a large comfortable chair in the den, he pulled out his list of questions. Slowly he unfolded it and began to read them again, silently to himself. Victor was sitting closest to Anatoly and noticed the paper he was reading. He leaned toward the boy and asked, "What do you have there, son?" Anatoly sat up straight, and just then the clock on the mantle chimed. They all knew what time it was, and Anatoly fully expected the two Russians to begin reciting the story of the history of the Leviathan. But they all looked toward the clock, had a moment of silence, and then turned their attention to Anatoly.

He began, "I have a list of questions about Leviathan. They looked at the Admiral, and the Admiral stretched out his hand toward Anatoly and made a motion with his fingers for Anatoly to come to him. Anatoly got up and walked over to PaPa, turned and stood between his knees. This gave him the confidence he needed. The Admiral took a sip of his drink then stated, "Anatoly I think you have everyone's undivided attention."

Anatoly began reading his list, "First question, what are your names? He said, "I know that," and scratched it from his list. "Two, are you going to find Leviathan?" Seth and Victor looked at each, then at the Admiral.

The Admiral said, "Anything said here this evening is strictly off the record and will not be divulged to the military or any other that it does not concern." Everyone was still quiet. The Admiral said, "I assure you, gentlemen, between the four of us even, if you wish." The Admiral told them of his correspondence with Anatoly and how he has not spoken of it to any for these years. He told them of Anatoly's young nanny, and her relationship, and that she had thought the Leviathan was just a story, that is until she came to Russia and visited the base with them. "That is the young teenage girl that visited the base, in the observation room with you and was by my side. Aryn is her name and she is sister to my assistant, Captain Mara Stacy Davis. And they would never break my trust for anything. They are like family, and frankly, we are all they have."

Before he could tell of Anatoly's plans, Anatoly blurted out, "I want to go with you back to the Antarctic."

The Admiral said, "Hold on Anatoly, I want to explain. I have told Anatoly of the harsh conditions and that he is much too young to go and survive. But obviously when he grows older he will go where he pleases and will know more of survival. And I will aid him in his pursuit if he still feels that strongly, when he is older."

The two Russians looked at each other one more time, and then sat back in their chairs, more comfortable with a sigh of relief. "Yes, we do have plans to find the Leviathan and to return to the city under the ice."

Anatoly excitedly blurted out "I knew it, I can help, I know how to find them, and I have gold we can use to pay." This outburst made them all to laugh and to be more comfortable. Seth looked again at Victor, as if to get approval, Victor nodded. Seth said, "We also have gold, a lot of it; and jewels, that we sold to fund the expedition."

The Admiral listened to all that was said between his young grandson and the two Russian men, and learned much. He was surprised at all that he learned. The two men began to tell of all their communication with the Leviathan. They reluctantly told how they aided in the escape of the Leviathan Queen and about the gold in the cave and their vessel loaded with the gold and supplies. They pointed out to the sea at the vessel they acquired. It was all lit up in the backdrop of the dark sea in the evening hours that were approaching rapidly.

The Admiral still sat quietly, taking it all in. The two men took turns expounding on the events that took place. "We met Lead Leviathan on the shore, and one by one they rose up out of the sea and followed Lead to the coordinates we gave him, to free the Queen, with no casualties, and minimal damages. When we were in the city under the ice, we fashioned horns of gold for their claws, to be left for us on this day. When summer in the Antarctic comes, our expedition will be ready to begin." Anatoly sat mesmerized at the new revelations unfolding before him. He could not speak a word, only thought in color of the events. Anatoly blurted out, "My gold is nothing compared to that."

When they finished, they looked to the Admiral and broke

the long silence with, "Admiral we don't mean to over step any boundaries with you or the Russian government, but we could not get any to see our goals. Except these few that serve us here and on the vessel, they believe in our cause and are going with us to deliver supplies and establish a colony. We were hoping to put money into your expedition that you might aid us in helping so many Leviathan to return into what they call home."

The Admiral was still speechless, sitting there, with his finger on his cheek, nodding his head.

Seth continued, "We were hoping, Admiral Voss, that you would approach our government to see if this was a possibility. But we also know they are afraid of the Leviathan and do not trust our assessments. It is because of the size and enormity of this creature they do not trust an alliance. But it is because of its size, we must trust an alliance for fear of retaliation. Though we do not believe they are capable. Just because they are equipped does not mean they will."

"We had many months of planning, when you pulled us from the icy prison. We were prepared with our backpacks full of jewels, which you did not inspect for all the excitement and confusion. The jewels funded this expedition thus far. We will find the Leviathan to make further plans, after they find their offspring somewhere in the Northern seas." Victor pointed out the window, North into the sea. Then Anatoly pointed in a more northeasterly direction and said, "More in that direction, Mr. Victor, sir." "Well, Anatoly, we still don't know how to find them."

Anatoly stood erect and started to get excited, "I know where to find them, I talked to Queen; well I did not talk to her, I, uh, made gestures and communicated parts of their story to her. She affirmed. I know how to find them.

Seth and Victor looked to the Admiral, and Anatoly turned and looked to him as well. The Admiral put his hands up and placed them on Anatoly's arms, looked him in the eyes for a long moment, then pulled him to his side. He looked past him, and began to speak to Seth and Victor in his usual authoritative manner. "Gentlemen let me get this straight. Leviathan came ashore here and rescued the

Leviathan we had chained and brought her back here? Then left you enough gold to fund ten expeditions. Technically, the jewels you brought back belonged to the Russian Government. So no one knows of the jewels and basically the gold was acquired separate from the military and no one knows about?" The Russians shook their heads.

The Admiral stood with his grandson in front of him and stated, "I guess we can organize a merger of our funds, equipment, and manpower; all need to be up to date. Finding a way is the problem. We must not tell anyone of our full intent. It seems our friends, the Leviathan are stealthy enough." The Admiral crossed his arms put his finger to his lips, looked to the floor, thinking. Then looking up as if his thoughts were renewed, he asked, "How large is your vessel?"

They all knew the adventure was to now begin. Seth and Victor laughed and stepped forward to shake hands with Admiral Voss and Anatoly. There was a lot of excitement and Seth got some plans of their vessel and brought it to the table with the ship's manifesto. They discussed the details of the vessel, the supplies they acquired, and the things of the environment of Lake Vostok, how it made them stronger and younger. There were other things they withheld from the Russian government for disbelief of the officials and because of the alliances they made with the Leviathan. It started to make sense to the Admiral why the Russians wanted to return, what provisions they had acquired, and what training the new inhabitants would require. It seemed to be too good to be true that the environment was so perfect. The Admiral was beginning to want to go live there himself.

"There is one thing Admiral," Victor began, "These seventy people that we have recruited to go, have not met a Leviathan face to face, though we have described its terrible visage, they just still think of Lake Vostok as a utopia. We need your expert advice on dealing with morale and preparing the people." "Can you talk to them?" Seth chimed in.

Anatoly perked up, he was getting tired. But when he heard this, he said, "See, PaPa, we could live there, the conditions are not harsh there. We could go. They need our help."

The Admiral looked from Anatoly, to the two men, scratched the back of his neck, and said, "You men are not making this easy on me." There was another minute of silence while everyone had his own thoughts.

The Admiral was thinking of problems and was the first to speak up, "These seventy people would be defecting. How would you deal with that?" Seth looked at Victor, pulled out an envelope for the seventy people and placed it in front of the Admiral. The Admiral said, "What is this?"

Victor stated, "We were hoping you could hire these seventy people, on a permanent basis, never to return from the Antarctic. These are all their credentials."

The Admiral turned, walked a few paces to the window, put his hand on his chin, and shook his head. Still looking out the window he said, "Like I said, you men are not making this easy for me." Then as if he was rejuvenated, the Admiral spun on his heals, turned about with the envelope in his left hand. He slapped it into the palm of his right and said, "Gentlemen, I will see what we can do." He stretched out his hand toward Anatoly and said, "Come, Grandson, we must get you home to bed."

Anatoly ran to catch up to his PaPa, taking him by his hand. Anatoly's small hand seemed to disappear in his GrandFather's grasp. As they headed for the door, Anatoly turned half about and said, "See you soon, Mr. Seth, Mr. Victor."

PaPa looked down and spoke to his grandson softly, "They have given us much to think about." The door was quickly opened for the Admiral, as they exited, he cut his eyes back to the two Russians that followed, and solemnly stated, "We will be in touch, very soon."

At this, the two Russians stood still, and watched them depart. When the door was opened, everyone outside came alive and began to scramble. The head of security walked half way up the walk to meet them, talking into his ear piece. It was late. The Admiral asked the head of security, "Did everyone get something to eat?"

He answered back, "Yes sir, we were well taken care of, and they served us all a very fine meal." The Admiral helped Anatoly into the vehicle, buckled him in, and closed the door. Anatoly leaned on the door and was instantly asleep.

The head of security got in the front and turned about as the Admiral got in next to Anatoly, in the back. "Admiral Voss, your daughter-in-law has been phoning all evening." The Admiral looked to him as if to say, "and?" So he continued, "I assured her the boy was safe with you in the house, and we would be returning directly." "Fine," the Admiral said in a tired voice. "Would you call her and tell her we are on the way, so maybe she can get some sleep." The head of security said, "Yes sir, right away." And he put up the window between the seats.

It was a quiet ride home from the coast. When they arrived, PaPa carried Anatoly to his room and put him in his bed carefully, as not to wake him. He touched him on his head and said, "Our little prodigy." Then he went to his room to rest.

CHAPTER 15

At Last

ANATOLY AWOKE IN HIS BED and tried to remember how he got there. PaPa carried him in the night and he didn't even wake up. It wasn't light outside yet. As not to wake anyone, Anatoly went quietly to his computer. He tried to draw a map…mapping out where the Leviathan might be or the proximity thereof.

As the sun came up, he heard some commotion in the kitchen and went in to see who got up first. It was Aryn. She decided she would make breakfast for everyone. She saw Anatoly and sung his name, "An na tolie." Anatoly sat on the stool, put his elbows on the counter and his hands on his face and just stared at Aryn. Aryn ignored him, as if she didn't see what he was doing and went about fixing breakfast.

"So, Anatoly, how did it go last night?" Anatoly acted like he didn't hear her, just staring a hole through her. "Anny!"

"Don't call me that. That's not my name!"

"Well!" Aryn exclaimed. "How did it go? You were awfully late coming home."

Anatoly sat up straight and put his hands down, trying to get a rise out of Aryn. He said, "We have a mission, another mission we must do."

Aryn looked kind of puzzled, thinking of where they were to go off on a mission. Not knowing any place around, she looked at Anatoly and said, "Who is going on a mission?"

Anatoly tsk, sighed and said, "Probably just you and me and PaPa and maybe Mara Stacy."

"Oh!" Aryn exclaimed. "And where is this mission?" She thought Mara Stacy had said she didn't have to go anywhere until she went back to the Antarctic in November.

Anatoly said, "I'm drawing a map if you want to see it."

"After breakfast, Anatoly, maybe after breakfast. Do you want to help?"

Anatoly put his elbows back on the counter and his hands on his cheeks and sighed a deep sigh.

Just then PaPa came around the corner. He was always dressed nice, and he was always wide awake. "Good morning, children," the Admiral exclaimed. "Oh, Aryn, you've got coffee made. Thank you very much."

"You're welcome, PaPa."

"What's this about a mission, Anatoly?" he queried as he sat on the stool next to him.

Anatoly sat up straight, put his hands by his side, and grabbed his stool with his fingers. "PaPa you know it's a secret mission."

He ignored him and drank a sip of his coffee.

Anatoly went on, "Can Mara Stacy and Aryn go with us?"

PaPa continued sipping his coffee and just kind of glanced down with his eyes at Anatoly. He could see Anatoly looking impatiently for an answer, but he never took his eyes off the coffee.

Aryn put the newspaper on the counter by the Admiral and asked him, "PaPa what is Anatoly talking about?"

"Well," PaPa started, "It's a mission that has been funded and that has made Anatoly and myself an integral part, an important part, and it looks like it cannot be done without us."

Anatoly started to get excited and bobbled about on his stool still holding his arms to his sides and holding on to the sides of the stool with his hands. He held his lips shut tight in anticipation of what PaPa would say next.

PaPa looked down at him with his eyes again. "It's more of a vacation and a pleasure cruise than it is a mission. Right, Anatoly?" Still with his lips tight, Anatoly answered PaPa with, "Mhum, Mhum." He started to bobble even more, the stool legs coming partially off the floor as he bobbled.

Aryn put their breakfast on the counter in front of the two of them. "A pleasure cruise? That sounds like fun," she said. "Who is it with?"

Anatoly could not contain himself any longer; he put his hands on the counter and said, "With Victor and Seth."

PaPa interrupted, he calmly said setting down his coffee cup, "It seems Anatoly has made quite close friends of the two affluent Russians that we rescued from the Antarctica. They have quite a large vessel at sea that they are going to cruise around the Northern Islands. We shall see if Anatoly's Mother and Father wish to go with us (knowing his Father would be working and his Mother would not get on a boat unless she had to, then she would take sleeping pills to sleep).

Just then Mara Stacy came dressed in her pressed uniform. As she came down the hall she exclaimed, "What smells so good?" knowing that it was Aryn making breakfast. She walked into the kitchen, put her arm around Aryn's shoulders and kissed her on the head, "Aryn, you have become so responsible. What are we discussing this morning?" and she turned to face Anatoly.

Anatoly still had his hands on the counter and tightened his lips, bobbling on his stool again.

Mara Stacy looked at the Admiral and said, "Admiral, what happened last night?" The Admiral lifted his eyebrows and as he took a sip of coffee, he said, "Happened, whatever do you mean?"

"Well, Mrs. Voss was very concerned that her son was out so late," said Mara Stacy.

The Admiral put his cup down, grabbed his utensils and said,

"She knows he is safe with me. Besides, the secret service told her the several times she called last night, that we were still at the Russian's home."

"Oh," Mara Stacy said. "Maybe I will see them today. I have to go to the base to conclude some paper work that was sent from the Antarctic."

The Admiral said, "I don't think you will see them anymore. They have retired. In fact, Captain Davis, they have secured a private vessel in which they wish all of us to go on…a pleasure cruise."

"Oh," Mara Stacy said, "Where to?"

The Admiral looked down at Anatoly and said, "Grandson, sit still and eat your food."

Anatoly started eating his food rapidly. He then looked up at Mara Stacy, back to his food, and back up again at her. He waited for PaPa's reply.

"More to the North of the Barents Sea, the Islands of the Barents Sea." Mara Stacy put one hand on her hip and started to pick up her coffee with her other hand. She raised one eyebrow and looked at the Admiral.

Knowing what was meant by the gesture and before she could say another word, the Admiral said, "When you go to the base today, put us in for a leave of absence for a few months so we can attend this pleasure cruise."

Mara Stacy tried to raise her one eyebrow even further, and said, "Admiral?" questioning.

The Admiral looked sternly back, and said "Captain," putting her in her place. Then he stated, "The necessary paperwork to take with you today is on the bureau in my room. You will file it today, won't you, Captain?"

Mara relaxed her composure and let out a deep sigh. All she could say was, "Yes Sir." They resolved the bit of tension in the room.

Aryn came up to her sister, put her arm around her waist and tugged on her a little, she said, "Come eat your breakfast, Mara Stacy. It sounds like we will have fun. PaPa said I could go with you. I will keep Anatoly in line."

Mara reached back, put her arm around Aryn, looking away from the Admiral, she said, "But who will keep the Admiral in line?" She turned to eat her breakfast.

Anatoly took advantage of the moment of silence and blurted out with food in his mouth, "It will be fun. It is an adventure. A new adventure." That made everyone smile.

A few weeks later, the details being worked out, everyone's fears subsided. They packed their bags and took a helicopter out to the Russian's vessel. It was a large vessel, they realized, a helicopter pad, lifeboats, very extravagant. As they landed, they were met by everyone on the deck. They had porters to take their bags.

The Russians turned to the porters and asked if they would show their guests to their rooms.

The Admiral went with the two Russians to the radio room as Anatoly, Aryn, and Mara Stacy were shown to their rooms which were quite stately. They had adjoining rooms with a door between.

"Wow, these are really nice rooms!" they all exclaimed at once. They unpacked their bags and Aryn heard a knock on her side door and opened it to find Anatoly standing there. "Let's go exploring!"

Aryn said, "Let's ask Mara Stacy." They turned to the door on the other side of the room that lead to Mara Stacy's room. She knocked on it. Mara Stacy answered the door, and there was Aryn standing there. She could see little legs standing behind Aryn. She bent over, reached around Aryn, grabbed Anatoly and tickled him under his arms.

Aryn said, "Anatoly wants to go exploring around the vessel. Do you want to go?"

Mara Stacy turned to finish unpacking. She said, "No, I'm going to the bridge to see the Captain to see if I can find out where exactly this vessel is taking us. You two stay out of trouble, and I'll see you at dinner."

Anatoly jumped out beside Aryn nudged Aryn with his arm and saluted, and Aryn did likewise, both of them said, "Yes ma'am. Anatoly did an about face, grabbed Aryn by the hand and pulled her backwards stumbling, and trooped off down the hall to see what they could find.

Aryn asked Anatoly, "I wish you'd get someone to show us around."

Anatoly said, "I already have a set of plans of the vessel from the Russians, and I know just what I'm looking for."

Aryn just tagged along looking at the sights, greeting everyone they passed. Everyone they passed had a smile on their face. Everyone was about their duties, acknowledging the children as they passed but paying no attention as to what they were doing. Down a hall, down the steps, through the galley, down another hall, down more steps, Aryn was being pulled along as much as possible.

Finally, she pulled back her hand and stopped. "Where are we going?"

Anatoly said, "Just a little further. I know it's here. I know it's here somewhere.

"What, what is it?"

Just then Anatoly came to a locked door. "A locked door, I knew it." He tried to get in, jiggling the lock. He said, Let's go ask for a key and they will give us a key."

"Why would they give us a key?" Aryn exclaimed, but she followed along behind Anatoly as he climbed back up the stairs, down the hall and to the bridge, where the Admiral sat.

Victor was looking at some charting maps and Captain Davis was conversing with some of the crew who spoke English, speaking to them in English and broken Russian.

He stopped at the door and Aryn pulled back her hand and said, "They are busy."

Seth heard them. He cut his eyes up towards the door. "Ah, Anatoly and Eran."

"Aryn," she corrected him.

"Aryn, please come." They came over to the table and looked at the charts there. They made no sense to Aryn. She knew nothing about charts.

Anatoly took out the protractor and the dividers, pretending to know as if he knew what he was doing. Maybe he did. No one knew.

He stopped, pointed with his finger. Touching the tip of his finger to a section of the map, he said, "Right here."

They all stood up, folded their arms, and looked at each other. The Admiral said, "I think the boy is right," speaking in Russian. The only one who didn't understand was Aryn. He marked the spot on the map. "Set a course to the very place Anatoly plotted out."

Seth said, "Well, you have saved us some time Anatoly. What is it that you want?"

Anatoly said, "I want the key."

Victor sat back in his chair and said, "The key?"

Anatoly firmly looked at Victor and said, "Yes, the key; I want to show my friend Aryn."

They looked at one another again.

Seth nodded to Victor.

He took the key out of his shirt from around his neck. He handed it to Anatoly. He put his finger to his mouth and did a "Shh" sound.

Anatoly put his index finger across his chest, held up three fingers on the same hand as if it was some kind of promise. He turned, grabbed Aryn by the hand and was off running again through the corridors, down the stairs.

Aryn was trying to catch up.

Anatoly waited for her at the bottom of the stairs each time.

"Anatoly," how did you know? How did you know they would give you the key?"

He walked much slower and took Aryn by the hand. He was leaning forward swinging the key around his neck. He stood up and said "Aryn, you have to promise."

Aryn stopped and put her hands on her hips. She stooped down to Anatoly, "Promise what?"

He said, "Promise not to tell anybody ever."

Aryn hesitatingly said, "I don't know."

Anatoly wheeled around and said, "Then stay here." He walked up two steps.

Aryn chased after him and said, "I promise, I promise." Aryn followed Anatoly back to the locked room. It was a strange sort of lock, the key went in at the bottom and the lock went all the way up half the door.

As Anatoly put the key in it and it made a big clinking sound. It was a large lock, worthy of such a key. He could only reach the bottom of it and said, "Aryn, will you take the lock off?"

She took the lock off and hooked it back on the hasp. The door was a heavy door but opened easily on its hinges. As the door creaked open, it was dark. As the light sprang in when the door opened, Anatoly said "Find the lights, find the lights!"

She felt along the wall on the inside. Aryn said, "Here it is, I found it." As she turned Anatoly back toward the middle of the room, Anatoly was running toward a pile of giant metal horns that was lying along in piles. Aryn stayed at the door looking.

Anatoly walked over to one of the first horns lying down and crawled into the end of it. Aryn shrieked, "Anatoly, don't!" He turned around inside of it and peered out, "They can't hurt you," he replied.

"What are they? What is this room? How did you know?" Aryn wasn't getting any answers.

Anatoly just played, crawling in and out and around. Anatoly found two pencils from the desk on the side of the wall. He began to beat on the horns like drums, walking from one to another, different sizes, slightly different shape, all of them made of metal. "They almost make music," Anatoly said, "We need some drum sticks for this."

Aryn bent down and looked inside of one of them. Aryn looked around the corner. It was smooth on the inside with grooves, shiny; very shiny on the inside. "Anatoly, what are these?"

"Gold," Anatoly simply replied.

"Gold?"

Aryn stood up looking puzzled.

Anatoly said, "Gold, solid gold."

"Gold, real gold, like gold, gold?" Aryn said.

Then looking about the room, they noticed that the back parts of the room were dim. Anatoly went back to the light switches and turned on the remainder of the lights exposing the rest of the room to the light.

Aryn realized then it was a very large room. It seemed to go on forever, and it was full of these golden horns, bigger than themselves.

Aryn stood there scratching her head, wondering, "How, what, where?"

Anatoly worked his way through the horns as if to be looking for something different. Anatoly said to Aryn, "Can you keep a secret, if I tell you?"

"I can, I will keep a secret," said Aryn.

Anatoly said, "Cross your heart." He made the motions to show her. She remembered that he did that up on the bridge to the Russians. "Who am I to keep the secret from, Anatoly?"

"Oh I don't know, maybe Mara Stacy, some of the crew, Mother and Father."

"Mother and Father? What about the Admiral?" Aryn queried.

Anatoly said with a tsk, "The Admiral knows of course; PaPa was there when they told us. Although he hasn't seen them yet, I knew they were here." The gold was so thick and it was spread out and used as ballasts in the ship.

Aryn still didn't understand. "Why are they shaped like this? Why are they so big and why are there so many? It's a fortune!"

Anatoly then started acting smart because he knew something Aryn didn't. "It's to afford an expedition," Anatoly spoke matter-of-factly.

Aryn asked Anatoly with a statement, "I suppose you know all about this expedition?"

Anatoly said, "I do, but I can't even tell you unless…." He walked around the corner hiding behind the horns so Aryn wouldn't see him for the next thing he wanted to say.

Aryn started to follow him and asked, "Unless what? Unless what? Anatoly come back, unless what?" Anatoly started running between the horns and around them, the piles, hiding from Aryn, until they started to play and laugh. Aryn anticipated which way Anatoly would go. He might be smart but he wasn't as good at hide-and-seek as Aryn was. She ran back the other way and caught him. When she picked him up, Anatoly caught her by the back of her head and kissed her right on the lips. Aryn dropped him on the ground astonished. "Anatoly." She stopped. She was in shock. "What did you do that for, Anatoly?"

Anatoly looked down at his feet, put his hands behind his back, shuffling his feet. He said, "I wanted your attention."

"You have it now. What is it?"

He said, "I want you to go with me."

She said, "I am with you. Where?"

Anatoly fumbled his feet together some more. He put his lips together and blew up his cheeks letting the air out in a puff, puff, puff. He looked up at Aryn. She was so much taller than him. They were so young. He said, "To Utopia."

Aryn's voice got soft, "Anatoly, there is no such place."

Anatoly quickly grabbed her wrists tighter and tried to pull her down to his level. "There is, there is such a place. It's all I've been thinking of."

Aryn said, "Anatoly, you are too little; you're too little."

He pulled harder on her arms. He said, "I won't be little forever, when I'm 20 it won't matter. I'll be bigger than you."

This sent Aryn into thinking about Anatoly like she never had before. She loves everything about him, she thought. But she's the nanny! She can't think of him differently, he's too little. She shook herself from her thoughts and said, "Where are you talking about? Where, Anatoly?"

He said, "I told you now. That's what these horns are paying for, to build Utopia. Everyone on this vessel knows about Utopia. That's why everyone is here. That's why they're helping. This is going to pay for it all. Utopia is already paid for, this boat, their house. That's where we are going…to find."(Anatoly stopped and thought to himself not to tell her that part). He closed his mouth, tightened his lips and let go of her arms.

Aryn stood up erect and slowly followed him as he shuffled his feet and slowly walked away from her around the corner. A thought slowly came to her mind. She knew Anatoly well, "Anatoly, what are you not telling me?" He kept walking away from her. She started to follow, "Anatoly, Anny!"

Anatoly started to run away from her. As he ran toward the door, he said "Don't' call me that!" and slammed the door behind him. He went back to his room and locked himself in. The key he left still in the lock. Aryn turned off the lights, turned the key in the lock, and locked it back. She went back towards the bridge. She walked slowly with her thoughts. She took the key back and handed it to Victor and said, "Thank you."

The Admiral sensed her complacency, said "Aryn." She stopped and turned back to him. He noticed her heading for the door... He said, "Where is Anatoly?"

She put her hand to her mouth, brushed her lips with her fingers and said, "In his room, I think. I'll go see." She turned and walked slowly to the door.

Captain Davis noticed that she came in, came to the table the Admiral was working at and asked, "What was that all about?"

The Admiral said, "I'm not sure."

Captain Davis said, "I will go find out," and she abruptly left the room.

They traveled for three days on calm seas. It was an uneventful trip, but very pleasant. Aryn and Anatoly kept their thoughts to themselves. As they approached the area, Anatoly was on the bridge with the two Russians and the Admiral. He had a type of navy hat and clothes on that his Mother had bought him. He was standing at the helm with the assistance of the helmsman. He pointed over to an icy patch on the peninsula and said "Over there at ten o'clock. Is that it?"

They looked at their gauges and maps and the other instruments. "I believe it is, Anatoly. I believe it is," said the Admiral. As they slowly pulled in towards the barrier peninsula, they barked out orders and weighed anchor. They let down a rather large boat. Anatoly, the two Russians, and the Admiral went by themselves to the icy island.

Anatoly insisted they take a large wooden chair he had found on the boat, though he wouldn't tell them why.

It was just about evening, the time in which the Leviathan would be telling their story. They got off onto the icy peninsula... Anatoly looked at the Admiral's watch and turned to the Russian. He said, "Now."

Victor said, "Now what?"

He said, "Get the chair, get the chair." He walked over to the boat and got the chair. He said, "Pick it up by the back and crush it on the ice near the water's edge. He did so and not understanding what was going on, they were kind of in a trance as Anatoly took charge. "Harder," he said. "Try to break it on the ice." He hit it again and again. Every few minutes, Anatoly would say, "Do it again, hit it again." The chair began to crack and break. It was a heavy wooden chair, but it could only take so much punishment.

Just then, emerging from the water, as if it was one great island, the backs and the heads and the tails of the whole Leviathan nation appeared, larger than the peninsula. They were so close together, they looked like one massive body. Everyone stood in awe.

Anatoly walked ahead to the shore's edge. Then the Leviathan split apart. One smaller Leviathan swam right in the middle of them until her head came right up to the icy edge, and the Leviathan did hold her up. Still astounded at what was transpiring, Anatoly acted as though he knew this would happen and he greeted the Queen with a bow and words in the Leviathan language. Then he turned to the two Russians and said in Russian, "Come closer." Still astounded at the sight and magnificence of what was transpiring before them they joined Anatoly.

Anatoly said, "Ask her."

"Ask her what?"

"The questions, of course," Anatoly said.

They asked of the part of the Leviathan nation of the North that were left behind so many years ago. Were they still alive? Were they still going to return to Antarctica, the icy palace? And many other questions the men tried to communicate to Queen.

They told them that they had the golden horns aboard the vessel and other provisions and that there were only thirty or so who were willing to go.

The crew of the ship was all standing on the ship's edge and could not tell what kind of island this was. They could see the four small figures in the distance on the white icy shore but they had no idea what was going on.

The two Russian men with Anatoly, were told it would be better to have a hundred. They agreed on many things.

Then as suddenly as the Leviathan appeared, the whole island of the Leviathan submerged into the icy sea.

LEVIATHAN AWAITS

INSPIRED BY MY CHILDREN.

ABOUT THE AUTHOR

Felic Jamison V. Fussner was born in 1962 in Richmond, Indiana. As a ten-year-old boy, he moved to Pensacola, Florida, where he now resides on a remote lost key, ever exploring the waterways with his ten children and eight grandchildren.